Lock Down Publications and Ca$h
Presents

BETRAYAL OF A G

A GANGSTA'S HONOR

I0564745

Written By
RAY VINCI

First Edition 2024

Printed in the United States of America

Lock Down Publications
P.O. Box 944
Stockbridge, GA 30281
www.lockdownpublications.com

Like our page on Facebook: Lock Down Publications
www.facebook.com/lockdownpublications.ldp

Stay Connected with Us!

Text **LOCKDOWN** to 22828 to stay up-to-date with new releases, sneak peaks, contests and more…

Like our page on Facebook:
Lock Down Publications

Join Lock Down Publications/The New Era Reading Group

Visit our website:
www.lockdownpublications.com

Follow us on Instagram:
Lock Down Publications

Email Us: We want to hear from you!

Acknowledgements

I would like to give a major shoutout to the greatest people in my life: Collen, Kemik, Astra, Myanell, and Annesha. With y'all's support I can do nothing but go to the top, which is the plan. Y'all been down since the beginning and I love each and every one of y'all till the death of me. To my mini me's Heaven and Za'yon, I do this for y'all. Y'all motivate me to drive for greatness so I can spoil y'all rotten, but I need y'all to me so much greater than me. I love you both. Shoutout to my boy Trey AKA (Bull) for taking care of me when I was down bad. Real recognize real. I love you bro. Shout out to my boy Adrian for giving me the stamps to send this book out you and Trey. It's crazy that the people you least expect will be all the motivation to you. To the whole Torres unit I feel like a superstar everywhere I go and stop asking to put y'all in my books. I see you niggas every day. I'm, not trying to think about y'all day. Y'all cool but y'all ain't that cool. Naw I love y'all and thanks for the support. And to my lil brother Robert we gon be good. Hop on the money train so we can take care of the fam. I need your help. I love you always.

Dedications

I know you thought I forgot about you, huh? I dedicate this book to the CEO of LockDown Publication, Ca$h. I'm still in awe of the day you took a chance on me. You believed in me when I didn't and when I was just writing a book because I felt I could. I finally said fuck it and sent you my first three chapters and everything else was a wrap. I also dedicate this book to all of the writers on Lock Down Publication. Stay motivated because it's easy to be sidetracked. I'm at a standstill and I lose focus until my Torres Unit fans get on my ass. Remember the game is ours. Holla at me on Facebook, or email me, or you can hit me up though mail. I promise to get back all of y'all. San Antonio stand up! We are finally in the building.

FB: Ray Vinci
Benny Hayward-Smallwood #01822689
You can JPay me for faster results.
125 Private Rd-4303
Hondo, TX 78861
Torre's Unit

Chapter 1

Peanut had just opened his eyes when he heard Big Mama on the other side of his bedroom door. "Boy, wake your behind up and come eat so you could get ready for church!"

Big Mama was in her early 60's, short with long, straight hair that went to the middle of her back, caramel complexion, and the weight of 120-pounds. She was strict but was also the sweetest person you could ever meet. She had been raising Peanut since his father was gunned down in front of Peanut's school while dropping him off.

His mother—the way her daughter had given up on life—was nowhere to be found since that day. At first it was easy because Peanut's father had left behind a chunk of money. But now, that was gone and Peanut was 17 years old and in high school. Things were getting harder.

Peanut raised out of bed, rubbed the sleep out of his eyes and headed for the bathroom. Once he got himself together, he got dressed, grabbed his phone, and then headed to the kitchen. "Good morning, Big Mama. You look beautiful, what's for breakfast?" He asked while giving her a kiss on her cheeks.

"Boy, sit down. That talk only works on those fast-tail girls. What took you so long to get ready? It's nine o-clock. We have to go in thirty minutes, so hurry up," she said while setting his plate in front of him. She sat down and said grace before they started eating. It was quiet until Big Mama broke the silence. "The only time you quiet is when you have one of those crazy dreams. You want to talk about it?"

"No ma'am," he said.

Peanut always had dreams about his father being killed by two men in black masks. Before the dream would end, it would switch to an all-white room with no one in it, just voices that he could barely understand. He could never figure out the voice because he would always wake up. He realized that he only had dreams like that when he had done wrong.

They had finished their breakfast, cleaned up and headed for the door. When they walked outside, it seemed like the whole housing complex was already awake and moving around. The Carson Homes was like its own little world. Everybody knew everybody.

As soon as him and Big Mama got to the car, he spotted Jay coming down the street. Peanut and Jay had been best friends since they were 10 years old, so they did everything together. Big Mama didn't like it one bit.

"What up, Peanut? Are you still coming to kick it at the crib or what?" Jay said while giving him dap.

"I'm try, but I might be busy. I'll call you later to let you know what's up," he said before his grandma could say something. Jay understood and changed the subject.

'Hi, Big Mama, how's everything going?' Jay asked Big Mama.

"I'm fine. When are you gon' bring your tail to church? You running around here with your pants halfway down your butt."

"Maybe next Sunday, I gotta handle some business so I gotta run. I'll catch up with you later, Peanut," he said as he took off.

Big Mama just shook her head as they got in the car and pulled out of the driveway. The ride to church was quiet except for Marvin Sapp playing through the radio. It took them fifteen minutes to get there. When they got there, the church had already started. The whole time Pastor James preached; Peanut was in a different world. Once church was over, Pastor James walked over to Big Mama and Peanut.

"Hey, Big Mama, how's life been treating you?" Pastor James asked.

"It's rough but we're making it through. I'm so proud of you. You've come a long way, Pastor," she said while giving him a hug.

"Thank you. Peanut, what's up? You alright?" He gave Peanut a concerned look.

"Yeah, Pastor, I'm good." He cut it short because he didn't want to hold a conversation. Pastor James was about to say more until his daughter Hazel walked up. Hazel was very beautiful, light skinned with hazel eyes. She had curly hair that went past her shoulders and a smile that would light up the night. She was 5 '1, weighed 125 pounds and people could only imagine what her frame was like.

"Hey daddy, can I spend a night over Mrs. Jones' house tonight with Jasmine?" She asked.

"Sure. I know you remember Big Mama. She used to watch you and that one right here," said Pastor James while looking at Peanut.

"Hey, Big Mama," she greeted. She really didn't remember Peanut because it had been so long ago but she always saw him at school or church.

She looked at Peanut and was at a loss of words because he was very handsome. Peanut stood at 5 '11, weighing 150 pounds with short wavy hair. He had a smooth dark-skinned complexion that the ladies loved. He had pearly white teeth and a sexy smile that showed off his dimples.

"Hello umm…." she said, waiting for his name.

"Oh, uh Michael but everybody calls me Peanut," he spoke.

"My name is Hazel. Nice meeting you. Well, daddy I have to go, my ride is waiting for me. I love you." She gave him a kiss and took off.

"Yeah, Pastor we have to go so Peanut can get ready for his basketball game tonight," Big Mama spoke.

"Oh yeah! Me and ya old man used to shoot around a little bit. Maybe me and the wife will stop by and watch."

"Okay, Pastor James," he said as him and Big Mama headed towards the car.

***

It was 6:00 pm and Peanut had exactly an hour until his game started. He had on his school sweats since they were already dark. He paced back and forth waiting on Jay to come back with the stolen car that he said he had. He already didn't want to go through with what was fixing to happen, but they had already been planning it for weeks. Right then, he was thinking about backing out. Jay had pulled up in an all-black Honda Civic with dark tinted windows. Jay rolled down the window and told him to jump in.

"Damn nigga, wat took you so long? I was thinking you got jammed for stealing the car," Peanut spat as he got into the car.

"No, I just had to make sure everything was everything so nothing would go wrong." Jay pulled off slow then headed towards the middle of the Eastside.

"Alright, when we get there don't get scary and shit because that's how shit gets fucked up," Jay said. Jay was the rough type, light skinned with green eyes and curly hair hung over his ear. People would always say Peanut was the brains of the two and Jay was the muscle. Most was right.

"Nigga I know, and I already got somebody on deck ready to get whatever we get."

"That's what I'm talking about. If this goes good, we'll be set for a lil while."

For the rest of the ride, they were both quiet. Peanut was praying and little did he know so was Jay. When they pulled up in front of an abandoned house, Peanut gave Jay a confused look.

"What's up?" Peanut asked.

"Look, I know I told you I was the only one with a gun, but I can't have you go in there naked," Jay said and handed him an all-black Glock 9mm.

"If it gets too hectic you know wat you gotta do."

"Yeah, let's just do this so I can get to my game."

They got out, headed down the street and the apartments were on the right. It was only a couple of people outside so they knew everything would go smooth. They walked by a few apartments before they got to the right one.

"You ready?" asked Jay.

Peanut nodded.

They both put on their ski masks, then pulled their hoodies over their heads. Jay knocked twice.

"What's up? What y'all need?" A big dude asked, opening the door.

"Everything y'all got in this bitch!" Jay pointed the gun in the big dude's face and shoved him inside.

Peanut moved in right behind Jay as if he had done this before.

"Look man, y'all can have everything. Just don't hurt me," the man pleaded.

"Where's the shit at, and who else is here?" asked Jay.

"It's two other people in the back with money and weed."

"Call 'em up front, and if they make any moves, yo' ass is dead!"

"Bobby, D, come here. Let me holla at y'all real quick!"

When Bobby and D came up front they were met by the barrel of Peanut's gun. Peanut and Jay tied all three men up and then shook down the house. Satisfied with what they found, they ran out the house and back to the car. They tossed the bags in the back seat and drove off to Sam Houston High School.

When they got to the school, it had just turned 7:00 p.m. and his team had just ran out to the court. He spotted Big Mama sitting next to Pastor James and his wife. He waved her way. Jay had gone to sit next to some girl and her friend that looked a lot like Hazel.

"Michael, pay attention. This is your first game so you better not lose!" His coach yelled at him.

Peanut was their starting point guard and also the star player on the team, so they really needed him in the game. He had to clear his mind, so he looked back at his grandma who looked so calm. As he stepped onto the court, all he thought about was playing ball. Everybody was cheering and yelling his name like he was already a superstar. When the game was over, Peanut went straight to the locker room, showered then he got dressed.

He had met Jay outside of the gym as soon as he came out.

"Nice game, baby boy. Eighteen points, eight assists, and eight rebounds, not bad. Look, I got these shorties tryna go eat. What's up? You down?' Jay asked.

"Yeah, but let's me ask Big Mama."

As soon as they stepped outside, they were met by Big Mama, Pastor James, Mrs. James, Hazel, Jasmine and Mrs. Johnson.

"Peanut nice game, son. You play just like your old man. You are going to be a star one day," Pastor James said.

"Thanks Pastor, I appreciate you for coming to watch. Big Mama, you think I can stay over Jay's house tonight and we can go to school from there?"

"Well, since you had a good game, sure. But you better be at school tomorrow.

"Okay." He kissed his grandma then headed towards Jay, Jasmine, and Hazel.

Chapter 2

Jay's house was identical to Peanut's so when he woke up it took him a few seconds to realize where he was. He looked at the time on his phone and it was 5:00 am. It was enough time to iron his school clothes and split up what they came up on last night when they hit that lick. By the time he ironed his clothes and got out of the shower, it was 6:00 am, and Jay was already splitting up the money and weed.

"Wat up homie? Wat we looking like?" He was referring to the money and weed.

"Shit, we got six hundred dollars a piece and three pounds of weed," he said excitedly. Jay handed Peanut his cut of the money and was about to spit the weed up until Peanut stopped him.

"Hold up! I can't have that weed in Big Mama's house. She'll trip out if she finds that. Just leave it here and when it's time to get rid of it, we get rid of it.

"Cool, you wanna smoke something before you get to school?" Jay asked Peanut.

"Naw man but meet me at the Barbara Jordan Center after school," he spoke as he left out of the door.

When he got to his bus stop, it was a few people he knew from school. So, he said what's up then waited for the bus. He still had twenty minutes until his bus showed up, so he went inside of Drop Zone and brought some tacos and lemonade.

When he came out, he overheard the boys that was waiting for the bus talking about buying some weed after school. He started to say something but was scared.

When the bus showed up, they all got on. A lot of people knew who he was because he was on the basketball team.

"What's up Nut, you gone be at the gym later on?" Chris asked.

Peanut knew Chris don't like him for several reasons. So, he was wondering why he was asking.

"Yeah, why?"

"Just wanna know if you gone bring that weak ass game along with you," he voiced then laughed at his own joke. The whole bus got quiet waiting on Peanut to say something back. Peanut smirked to himself. He was quiet but decided to show off a little bit.

"If my game is so weak, how come I took yo starting spot? Oh, because yo lame ass can't win no games."

Everybody on the bus stood up and busted out laughing and Chris didn't like it.

"How about you go get ya best five and we can see who the best is, bitch ass nigga."

"I only play for money. How about two hundred dollars a player or is that too much for yo broke ass?" Peanut boasted.

"That's a bet nigga!"

Before Peanut could throw another assault back, his phone rung. He was going to ignore it until he saw that it was Big Mama.

"Hey grandma, you okay?"

"Yeah baby, just making sure you made it to school on time," Big Mama called.

"Yes ma'am, I'm on my way right now. I'll be home as soon as I leave the gym."

"Okay, you be careful!" She said as she hung up.

They had pulled up to the school and before he got off the bus, he texted Jay and told him about the bet he had with Chris. When he got off of the bus, everybody was standing around talking. He said what's up to the people he knew then went straight to his first period class. He tried to concentrate on his work but couldn't because his mind was on making money.

Peanut and Big Mama had been struggling to maintain the bills and keep food in the house, so he had made a vow to help his grandma anyway he could. It seemed like time was going slow and he couldn't wait to start making money, so he started putting a plan together. The bell for last period had rung and Peanut hurried up and grabbed his things then left out of class. Before he could make it out of the school, he heard a female voice call his name.

"Peanut, hold up!"

When he turned around, he saw one of the prettiest girls he'd ever saw at school. She was Puerto Rican with long black curly hair, dark skinned and a killer smile. She was 5 '6 and weighed 135 pounds all ass and titties. She was a head turner for sure but rarely messed with anybody.

"What's up, do I know you?" Peanut asked, looking her up and down.

She liked when he did that, so she smiled. "I was hoping so, but maybe we can get to know each other."

"Yes, we can. What's your name, lil mama?" He asked.

"Erica."

"That name fits you. Look, let's exchange numbers and maybe we can hook up later."

"Okay," she said as they exchanged numbers then they went their separate ways,

"Oh yeah, I'll see you tonight at your little game. Y'all better win, I got money on you."

All Peanut could do was smile and shake his head. He looked at her ass until she disappeared around the corner. Once he was outside, Jay was waiting in his mom's car, turned up the Gunna that was playing then drove off. Peanut's mind was on money the whole drive there. He was snapped out of his thoughts when Jay hit his arm.

"Damn nigga, we here. You must have been on Mars or something. You good or wat homie?"

"Yeah, I'm good, bro." Peanut voiced. They jumped out of the car, and he walked inside of the gym. Once they got inside, it seemed like the whole school was there as money was being passed everywhere. Try, Papa. Bubba D and EJ were waiting on the court as they went to the middle of the court to meet Chris and his squad.

"What's up, Nut? You sure you wanna lose ya lil money in front of everybody?" Chris asked.

"If you wanna up the money feel free homie." Jay spoke.

Chris laughed. Dre came and collected everybody's money.

As Peanut's squad prepared to get the ball inbounds, he spotted Erica standing up by the doors. He winked at her as he got the ball then dribbled down the court. He crossed over Chris with ease then threw Trey an alley oop. When he did that, the whole gym exploded in ohs. The whole game Peanut was scoring on Chris, and he didn't like it. Chris started roughing up Peanut and Jay, which was right up Jay's alley. Peanut passed Jay the ball then he drove right into Chris. Chris slid out of bounds into the wall and hit his head.

"Watch how you handle my homie, bitch as nigga!" Jay gritted through clenched teeth. Chris got up and finished playing but ended up losing.

"I guess I'm the best since yo scrap ass lost," Peanut said to Chris as him and his team collected their money from Dre. He could tell that Chris was salty about the loss. He made a mental note to pay close attention to him. After he collected his money, him and Jay headed towards the door. When he got there, he saw Erica counting up the money she had won.

"I guess you won yo lil bet. How much money did you win?" He asked her.

"Not much. Damn, I didn't know your game was tight like that, Papi."

"It's alright. Since I helped win that money, where is my cut?" He asked jokingly.

"Well, how about I buy you lunch tomorrow?"

"Cool, I gotta go. My ride is about to leave. If you want, we can drop you off."

"Naw, I'm good. I got my own car," she said in a strong Spanish accent.

"Okay, big baller I'll catch you at school." He gave her a hug then took off running. When Peanut made it to the car, Jay had full circle around him. Jay had everybody that was in the gym buying weed from him. Peanut was surprised that Jay even had the weed on him.

"What's up, Jay? You gotta be stupid to be selling that shit out here in the opening. What's yo problem?" Peanut called with anger in his voice.

"Wat you mean? Nigga I'm out her getting this money. This shit some fire because niggas buying this shit left and right." Jay boasted. Peanut couldn't even be mad, so he leaned up against the car until the circle cleared out. When everybody left, they both jumped into the car then drove off.

"What's up with that plan you had?" Jay asked.

"I was thinking instead of being out in the opening selling that shit, we could cop a spot and be low key. I can't let Big Mama find out and you can't let yo T-lady find out or we both dead. If we sell the rest of what we got, we'll be able to cop some more Killa and a lil spot to get rid of it." Peanut explained. "We'll still stay at our house unless it's pumping, but we never sleep where we shit."

Jay was liking what he was hearing so he was nodding his head as he drove.

"Okay, I like what I'm hearing but we have one little problem," Jay stated.

"What's that?"

"How we gone get the spot we both too young and we ain't got no IDs?"

"Just sell the rest of that Killa and I'll handle the rest," said Peanut.

Jay had pulled up to Peanut's house then parked waiting to see if it was more to Peanut's plan.

"How much money do you have all together?" Peanut asked Jay.

"With all the money from yesterday and today, a little over a band, why?"

"Okay, save everything you make. In a day or two, I'ma holla at Qball to see if he could get us some good prices on some more weed. Then, I'ma try to find somebody to cop us a spot," he stated as he gave Jay dap then hopped out of the car. He knew Big Mama was still up because the kitchen light was still on. Plus, it was only 8:00 pm. He stood on the porch and watched Jay pull off, and he couldn't wait until he put his plan in motion.

When he walked in, Big Mama was making him a plate. She made sure he always had something to eat when he came home. He loved his grandma and wished that his mom cared about him as much as she did.

"Hey grandma." He gave her a hug and kiss before he sat down.

"Hey baby, how was school today?"

"It was good. What's for dinner?" Peanut asked.

"Chicken, green beans, corn, and mashed potatoes," she said while sitting his plate in front of him.

He said his grace then went straight to work and Big Mama could do nothing but smile. As soon as he finished, his phone started ringing. When he realized it was Ericka, he answered. "I must be on your mind heavy because I just saw you," he said through the phone.

"I just called to say thanks for helping me win that money today," she spoke laughing.

"Oh, that's cool."

"No, I was calling to tell you goodnight, Papi and I'm looking forward to seeing you tomorrow."

"That's more like it and good night to you too, beautiful."

"Well, I'll see you later. I'll call you in the morning," she stated before she hung up.

Peanut said goodnight to his grandma then went to his room and called it a night.

Chapter 3

Peanut had woken up with money on his mind, and whoever planned on spending it, he was willing to make it. When he got to school, Erica was waiting on him by his locker.

"Hey Papi," she said while giving him a hug.

"I can get used to this," he stated while holding her. Before they could get into their conversation, two dudes walked up to Peanut. Peanut, growing up in the Carson Homes, was already in a fighting stance.

"What's up, you Peanut?" One of the dudes asked.

"Yeah, why What's up? You good homie?" Peanut asked, making sure everything was good.

"Jay told me to holla at you about some of that fire he had last night after the game."

He looked at Erica because he didn't want her to know what he did. When she gave him an approving look, he got straight to the business.

"Yeah, I do, but I don't have none on me right now, but shoot me your number and by lunch time, I'll hit you up when I got it." He explained.

"Okay, my name is Ray Ray. Just hit me up when you got it," he said then rattled his number off. Peanut had dapped him up then finished putting his number in his phone. Once he finished, he dialed Jay's number.

"Wat up, gangsta. Talk to me," Jay answered on the other end of the phone.

"Where y'all at? I need some of that Killa up here."

"I don't have a ride right now, but if you find a way. I'm at my cousin's spot off E-Commerce in the village."

"Cool, I'ma try to find a way so don't go anywhere," he said then hung up. He immediately started looking through his phone to see how he could call for a ride and came up with nothing.

"Damn!" He said to himself.

"What's wrong, Papi?" Erica asked.

He forgot Erica was even there, so she startled him.

"Nothing, just tryna find a ride so I can go pick up that Killa."

"Well, I can take you," she stated.

That caught him off guard because he had forgotten she had a car. Plus, he didn't want to get her involved with what he had going on.

"You're sure? I promise I'll put some gas in your car," he spoke excitedly.

"Yeah, just smoke some of that gas with me."

"Cool, let's go before my homie leaves."

They both snuck out of the side door where her red 2022 Toyota Camry was parked. Before he got in, he looked at her with surprise, because he wondered how she had gotten a ride like this. As soon as they got in, she peeled out of the parking lot.

"I know you know where the Village is at, right?" He asked.

"Yeah, I know."

"Okay, where did you get a fat ass ride like this at?"

"My grandpa spoils me, so I begged him for a car."

"Wat does he do for a living?"

She looked him up and down before she answered his question. "He owns Spanish restaurants."

He nodded his head with no reply.

"Wat's up with you? How long have you been selling weed?" She asked.

"Just started. I came across a few pounds and since I needed the money, I started getting rid of it." He explained.

They talked and got to know each other the whole ride and he realized that she was really cool. They pulled up, then he hopped out to go get what he needed. It took him fifteen minutes to go in and come out.

"My bad if I took so long, I just had to roll up a couple of sweets for the ride back, " he said as he got in and handed her two blunts. She wasted no time in lighting one of them up. She hit it a few times then passed it to Peanut. Erica started the car up then made her way out of the apartments, at the same. Peanut texted Ray Ray to let him know that he was ready.

"Wat are you gone be doing after school, Papi?" She asked.

"Probably try and get rid of this Killa so I can put my plans together, why?"

"Well, I just wanted to spend a lil time with you. I enjoyed our lil ride," she voiced as she made the turn on the street where the school was.

"If you want you can stop by my house later on or something, we can chill."

"Cool, but how about I drop you off at home after school."

"Okay, but once you find out where I stay, don't be on no stalking shit," he said as he laughed.

She said something in Spanish as they were getting out of the car. They said their goodbyes, gave each other a hug then promised to see each other later.

***

Things had been moving smooth for the last couple of days, so Peanut had decided to spend the day with Big Mama.

"Boy, it don't take that long to get dressed. Hurry up because Pastor James is waiting on us!" Big Mama yelled from the living room. Pastor James had invited her and Peanut over for lunch and she took the offer. She took it as a moment for him to get to know his dad's best friend and his family. Peanut had come out looking handsome and fly as hell in his gray 501 Levi Jeans, black V-Neck T-shirt, and some cool gray Retro 11 Jordans. To top it off, he had a fresh taper fade with his waves hitting all around. All Big Mama could do was smile because she saw a reflection of his dad.

"Come on, child," she said as they walked out of the door. They said their hellos and byes to their neighbors as they pulled out of the driveway. Big Mama and Peanut usually talked about everything but today he was texting on his phone, so she broke the silence.

"So, how is school?"

"It's good, and the team is winning more games," he said still with his face in the phone. She could tell the change in him, so she just left it alone. Hopefully, Pastor James could talk some sense into him. She realized that he was becoming a man and needed a father figure in his life. Pastor James had a house on the Northwest side, so it took them 20 minutes to get there. Peanut had never been to Pastor James' house so when he saw the two-story house, it caught him by surprise.

"Pastor James stays here? I didn't know Pastors had money like that," he stated as he continued to stare at the house.

Big Mama just shook her head as they both got out. As they walked up the driveway, Mrs. James had opened the door and greeted them. Mrs. James was a beautiful woman and Peanut had to look twice, and now he knew where Hazel got her looks from.

"Pastor is in the living room waiting on the game to come on if you want to watch," she said to Peanut then motioned towards the living room. On his way, he saw Hazel there, so he was caught by surprise and didn't realize he was staring until she said something.

"Hello! Earth to Michael!" She said sarcastically.

"Oh, my bad. I was in a zone. How are you doing, Hazel?" He asked.

"I'm fine. I didn't know you was coming," she voiced while trying not to look at him too long. She thought Peanut was cute, but he also had another side to him, which was one of the reasons she liked him.

"Well, I'ma go watch the game with your old man. I'll catch you later, huh."

"Okay." She left so quickly that it made him laugh. When he had gotten to the living room, the game had just started, and the San Antonio Spurs had just scored on the L.A. Lakers.

"Wat's up, Pastor? You mind if I watch the game with you?"

"Sure, I didn't know y'all was here already," Pastor James said as he stood up to greet Peanut. When he saw Peanut, his memory had shot back to when him and Grey had just started coming up. At that moment, he had decided to pay close attention to him.

"Who are you going for?" Pastor asked.

"Who else? The Spurs, five-time champs!" He boasted. They both was cheering and having fun until halfway through the second quarter when Hazel came in.

"Lunch is ready," she stated quick then left back out. They were both disappointed but knew not to question it. When they walked in the kitchen, the table was already set up as they sat down, and without him realizing, they sat next to Hazel. The whole time everybody was talking about everything. Peanut was barely paying attention to Big Mama and Pastor James because he and Hazel were laughing at what he did, but he did catch bits and pieces.

When everything was said and done, Pastor James had asked to speak to him on the back porch. Big Mama and Mrs.

James already knew what they were about to talk about, but Hazel was confused. They left the ladies as they headed out back to talk. Pastor James wasted no time and got straight to the point.

"So, how much do you know about me and your daddy's friendship?"

"I just know that y'all was best friends. That's it," said Peanut with a confused look on his face.

"Look, I know how it is when it's hard. Trust me, I've been there before, me and your dad. Me and ya pops use run these streets back in the day until things got real. Things started changing for a lot of people. Some people didn't like it and most had no choice but to deal with it. I know what you got going on. I ain't knocking it, but I don't want you messing up your career like we did." He explained. It seems life the more he explained, the more Peanut got mad. He wasn't expecting to hear none of this today.

"Your old man got killed doing the same shit you're doing, and I just don't want you to end up in the same way!" He yelled sounding like he was still in the streets.

"Oh, so now you think you know me. Who the fuck do you think you is, homie?" He asked as he let his temper show. "I know Big Mama put you up to this!" He turned and walked back in the house. He walked in and out through the front door so fast that all the women could do was stare in shock. Peanut didn't think about Big Mama; he just kept walking down the street. It seemed like everything had finally hit him and knocked all of his wind out. He needed someone to talk to and she dialed Erica's number.

"Hey Papi, What's up?" she said, sounding happy to hear his voice.

"Where are you at? I need you to come pick me up."

"What's wrong baby, are you okay?" She asked once she heard the anger in his voice.

"I'll tell you later. I'm on Ingram Road. Just meet me at Ingram Mall."

"Okay," she said, then hung up.

He had to calm down, so it was best that he stay away for a couple of days.

Chapter 4

Peanut had been spending a lot of time at Jay's house, so it was only right that he bought new clothes. He stepped onto the porch in some camo cargo shorts, a black V-Neck T-shirt, all black Air Force Ones, and a camo fitted cap. Things were going good for him and Jay but they was still looking for a connect and a place to get rid of the weed. Jay had stepped outside right behind Peanut in just a muscle shirt, basketball shorts, and some Debo house shoes. As soon as they stepped out, Q-Ball had just pulled up in a '88 Delta. When Q-Ball pulled up, Peanut and Jay looked at each other in confusion because Q-Ball rarely came to any one of their houses.

They both walked to the car as Q-Ball stepped out and sat on the hood of the car.

"What's up, homie? Wat brings you around the block?" Peanut asked as he shook Q-Ball's hand.

"Yeah, you never leave yo block," said Jay.

Q-Ball was tall and had muscles everywhere with braids that hung down to his shoulders. His dark skin hardly showed off his tattoos. You could barely see them.

"Naw, I just dropped by to let y'all know I'ma shoot somebody y'all's way so be ready. And I got somebody to get a lil spot in the back."

"Hell yeah, that's wat I'm talking about homie!" Jay said loud and excitedly.

Peanut sat quiet, thinking about how to put things in motion. "Who do you have to get us the spot, and how much does it cost?" Peanut asked.

"She should drop by later on and then y'all can deal with her. From now on, y'all business is with them not me," he said as he got back in his car. It took him no time to pull off and bend the corner.

Peanut and Jay took off to the back room then quickly started counting up their cash.

"How much do you got?" Peanut asked him.

"I got a lil bit over a rack. Wat you got?"

"About the same thing. We should have enough for the weed and the house. We might be broke for a lil bit, but it will be well worth it," spoke Peanut.

"How we gonna do this once we get everything?" Asked Jay as they put their money away.

Peanut had already been thinking about that, so he shot back with the answer quick. "Everything we make, we put back into our score fare and the house until we have enough money for ourselves. We go half on everything after that. Once we get the trap set up, we got to give everybody our numbers and then we take it from there," Peanut voiced as finished explaining himself.

Jay was amazed at how his homie was putting everything together. He knew if they kept it up, they would be making big moves in no time. At the same time, he knew once they started making big moves niggas would start hating. At that moment, he decided to put a squad together. Jay was deep in thought until his phone snapped him back.

"Wat up? Talk to me," said Jay through the phone.

"Yeah, this Mimi. I'm looking for Jay or Peanut."

"This Jay, wat you want?"

"Q-Ball told me about y'all situation with a house."

"Oh, okay. Shoot to my crib and we can work something out. You know where I stay at or wat?"

"Yeah, give me about twenty minutes," she spoke then hung up.

"Who was that?" Asked Peanut.

"Ol' girl that's gone get us the spot. She said give her about twenty minutes and she'll be over."

They both got happy then started giving each other dap. Everything was starting to fall in place for them and they knew once they were in, there was no turning back. Peanut had been waiting for this moment since they had first hit the lick on the weed, and now all he could think about was how things were starting to move fast. Right when he was about to voice his opinion to Jay, his phone rang. He looked from this phone to Jay with confusion because he didn't recognize the number. He shrugged, then picked it up anyway.

"Yeah, what up?" He said through the phone.

"Am I speaking with Peanut?"

"Yeah, but who's asking?" He shot back.

"Okay, I'm Los, Q-Ball told me to get up with you about some business. Do you want to meet up?" Said Los.

"Um yeah, but I'm kinda busy right now. We can meet up tomorrow at Johnny's around 12:00 pm."

Jay was still looking confused because Peanut wasn't telling him who it was, so he threw his hands up.

"Guess who that was?"

"Better had been Oprah by the way you were ignoring me." Jay shot back.

'Naw nigga, the new connect. We gon' meet up at Johnny's tomorrow and talk business," Peanut said while showing all 32 teeth.

"Why tomorrow when we got today?"

Peanut learned from his daddy to always stay in control of a situation, never move too fast, and you'll last a lot longer.

"Because we gotta handle that situation with Mimi."

"Oh yeah," Jay said as he lit up a blunt and headed towards the front porch. When they got outside, everybody was starting to wake up. Peanut looked around and immediately started thinking about Big Mama. He made a mental note to call and check up on her later on. He reached and grabbed the blunt from Jay and he could tell a lot was on his mind. He was gon' ask him about it but decided not to.

As he hit the blunt, a beat up 2004 blue Kia Rio pulled up. Out of being paranoid, Peanut reached under his shirt and they both stood up. Since the windows were tinted, they both looked confused but neither one said nothing.

When the driver side door opened and a beautiful chocolate female stepped out, they were even more confused.

"Hey, I'm looking for Jay!" She yelled at them.

"Yeah, wat's up?" Jay asked.

"I'm Mimi. I just talked to you on the phone."

"Yeah, yeah, come in so we can talk," he said. "Damn Mimi looks good," He spoke to Peanut.

When she stepped from around the car, Jay's mouth dropped because she looked like she jumped straight off of a T.V. show. She was 5'4", 115 pounds. You could tell she worked out because you could see every curve on her body. She wore a blue denim skirt with a white blouse and Dolce & Gabbana sunglasses on top of her head. The way she walked and the movement of her hips you could tell she had an ass to match titties. As she walked up, they could tell that something was different about her.

When she got to them, she looked them both up and down. "We gon get down to business or what?"

"Yeah, sit down," Jay said.

As she sat down, her eyes roamed from Jay to Peanut.

"And who are you?" She asked.

"Peanut." He kept is short.

"So, wat's up lil mama? What you got planned?" She said to Jay. "I'm not tripping on getting y'all lil ol' spot, but it's gone cost y'all."

"How much?" Peanut jumped in because he knew it was always a catch to every situation.

She shot him a quick glance out the corner of her eye before she turned and gave him her full attention. Peanut liked the way she was trying to keep control of the situation and knew what type of female he was dealing with.

"Just like y'all got a situation, I'm also in a pretty fucked up one my damn self. Me and my sister needs a place to stay and seeing that y'all need a place to do y'all's thing, I think what I'm charging is an even trade."

"So, you get us the spot and you are staying there," said Jay.

"Yeah, pretty much."

"I don't know. You might be a serial killer or some shit like that," Peanut said with a slight smile to let her know she was all good. To his surprise, she started laughing.

"Even if I was, it looks like you could handle yourself anyway," she said pointing at the gun she saw Peanut reach for earlier. "Shit if y'all got time, we can get rid of her and start looking."

"Alright, let me get dressed and we can burn off," he said as he and Peanut walked in the house, and she walked to the car.

***

When she got back in her car, her sister looked at her crazy because she didn't know what was going on. Mimi had just turned 18 years old, and her sister was 15 years old. She had been taking care of them both since she was 15 because her mom and dad passed away. Since then, they were living wherever they could.

"Look, these people are going to get us a place that we can live in. Something might go on in there, but it's cool. We'll just be grateful," Mimi said.

"Okay, but they look young. How can they help?" Asked Diamond.

"They are young. Y'all are the same age, and they know how to make money."

Diamond was brown skin with light brown eyes. Her hair was dark black and went right below the ear. She stood at 5'1 and with 110 pounds. She was barely stepping into new womanhood, and you could tell by how she was stacked with ass and titties.

Before they could continue with their conversation, Peanut and Jay walked out and headed toward the car. She knew what her sister was thinking because she thought the same thing. They both were young, but she knew that they both would be making boss moves. As they got closer, Peanut headed toward the backseat and Jay headed to the front. When Jay looked, he saw another female in the front, and he got in the back.

"My bad, lil mama. I didn't know you were in there," said Jay.

"Peanut, Jay, this is my sister, Diamond." She introduced and drove off. They drove around the neighborhood looking for a house and Peanut thought about the situation the girls were in. Him and Big Mama was struggling but they did have a roof forever over their head and a place to sleep. He was deep in thought when Jay hit his shoulder to snap him out of it.

"Damn nigga, you on Mars or something?" Jay asked.

"Naw, wat's up?"

"What about this house right there?" Mimi asked.

The house sat on the corner of Bee Street, and you could see down each street which made it the perfect spot.

"Yeah, it's perfect," They both said at the same time.

She put the number in their phone and drove back to Jay's house. On the ride back, they chopped it up a bit and got to know each other. When they pulled back up, Jay was the first one to hop out.

"Tomorrow, I'ma let y'all know how much I need for the house," Mimi said.

"Cool, thanks for what you doing. Look, wait right here real quick. I'll be back," said Peanut. Peanut got out, ran in the house and came right back out. He went to the driver's side and gave her some money.

"Here is two hundred dollars. This is not much but get y'all a room and something to eat."

"Thanks, Peanut."

He just walked off without saying anything.

She didn't know how he knew they were hungry and didn't have anywhere to go for the night but he did. She had gained a lot of respect for Peanut, and she knew then that she would help him to the end.

Chapter 5

He looked out of his office window from the second story and saw a black Navigator pull up to the gate. The guard buzzed him in because he knew who it was as well as he did. The Navigator pulled up in the driveway and he smiled at his nephew as he went out. His nephew had been in San Antonio for a little over 3 years and proved himself well. He came from Puerto Rico with money on his mind and now he was getting plenty. He heard a knock on the door and he turned around to wave his nephew in. He took a seat behind his desk and lit up a cigar as his nephew did on the same opposite side.

"Los, Sabrino, what brings you so early in the morning?" Cesar asked as he looked at his watch.

"Uncle, you know the only reason I'm here so early is because of money," Los said with a smile.

Caesar loved his nephew's way of thinking; it was like it was in his blood to be a boss. He'd hoped that one day he could leave the business to him and just do the right thing all the way.

"What's on your mind?"

"I got some new guys I'm meeting up with later on. From what I know they are young, and hungry. How should I feed them?" Los said while blowing smoke out.

Cesar sat back and thought for a while. He stood up and walked towards the minibar and poured him a shot of tequila. Cesar stood to at 6'1 200 pounds and was older so you could tell he was getting tired. He was dark complected with salt and pepper hair, and a few wrinkles in his face. He wore a black Armani suit, with black Armani dress shoes, a gold Swiss watch, and gold nugget pinky ring.

"Feed them good and treat them like family. Two hundred a pound and the good stuff too," he said.

"If it don't work out, pull back A-S-A-P."

"Okay, do I give it to them up front first to see what he is doing?" Los asked.

"It's up to you. Whatever you choose. This is your situation. Handle it right."

Los gave his uncle a handshake and a hug then walked out. He was excited because his uncle was trusting him more and more. He reached his truck in no time. He had one more stop to make which wasn't not far before he met with Peanut. Los jumped in his truck, turned up his music and drove off. Once he got outside, he pulled out his phone and dialed a number.

"Hey Papi, I'm on my way to get some of those things ready," he said and hung up.

It took him 10 minutes to get to Ingram Road due to the traffic. When he got there, who he had come to see was waiting outside for him. Los turned the music down out of respect for the neighbors. As he stepped out of his Navigator, old boy came to meet him halfway. He was half black, half Puerto Rican but look mostly black. He was tall with waves all around his head and a full beard that was trimmed low.

"Hey Papi, how is goes?" Los asked.

"You know everything's gravy. I just sent the wife and daughter to the mall so we could handle business. If they find out I'm still in the game, it's gonna be World War III," he said while laughing.

"Well, let's get moving. I gotta handle some business."

They walked to the back of the house and went to the shed. He opened it up and pulled a hatch that went to a downstairs chamber. He went down and came back with small duffle bag. Los unzipped it and saw five pounds of weed and was satisfied. They said their goodbyes and Los took off. He got on the freeway and headed towards the East Side.

"Hey Papi, I'm on my way, give me 20 minutes." Los said through the phone.

"Okay, call me when you get close," he said and hung up. Peanut and Erica were sitting in Johnny's eating tacos. They had just opened up and plus, he wanted to spend a little time with Erica for lunch. He had planned on making the drive then going back to school, but it didn't look like Jay was going to show up. His plans were changing. He picked up his phone and text Mimi to meet him at Johnny's in an hour. When she replied back okay, he was satisfied.

"Baby girl, I gotta handle some business here in a lil bit and I don't want you around." He told Erica.

"Okay, Papi. I gotta get back to school anyway. If I don't see at school, I'll be at your game tonight," she spoke as she got up. "Good luck, papi."

He was starting to cut for Erica real bad. He knew she was a rider. She never questioned him about this whereabouts or about his business. He looked at his phone because he'd got a text from a number he didn't recognize. The text said,

Are you okay? Haven't seen you at school or church lately.

He smiled because he knew it was Hazel. She was right so he hit her back and told her he was okay and he promised to be in church Sunday.

He heard the door open to the restaurant and looked up from his phone. He saw a tall, Spanish dude walk in. He could tell it was Los by how he dressed. He was dressed in Khaki slacks, a white dress shirt, some Stacey Adams and a coat that looked way too expensive for his taste. He was dark skinned with real straight hair that laid down on his head. He was skinny and could eat a few tacos himself. Los looked his way and they both gave each other a head nod to acknowledge one another. Los decided to walk over to his table since it was already in the back. He sat down and Peanut waved the waitress over to clean the mess him and Erica made.

"I see you already had company. Where's your partner at?" He asked.

"He had business to handle elsewhere, but I'm the one who handles business on this end."

Los liked Peanut already because he had the trait of a boss.

"Okay, talk to me, Papi."

Peanut had to smirk because Erica called him that, so he guessed Los to be Puerto Rican.

"Look, me and my partner came up with a few pounds of Killa and got rid of it pretty quick. Now, we have a lot of people willing to get whatever we get off of our hands, but the thing is we have no source for getting it," Peanut said without giving him a chance to speak. He learned from his daddy that always keep your man thinking and you'll get him everything. "I got a million-dollar spot and I'm trying make every penny that comes through it, and at the same time, give you a lil bit of it.

Los was liking how the kid was thinking. For a youngster, he had a lot of potential, and he was gone give him a chance to prove himself. Los nodded his head and started rubbing his chin to show his approval. "I like the way you talk, and I like the way you carry yourself. Now, tell me your proposition and I'll tell you what I can do for you."

Peanut liked having the ball in his court, but he knew Los was trying to see what he would do with it. "Look, I got a rack on me right now for starters, but I promise that I'll be sending so much money your way that you'll get tired of seeing it," voiced Peanut.

All Los could who was laugh because nobody could ever get tired of money, but with that, he made his decision. "Alright kid, I like you. You remind me of when I was growing up. This is what I'm going to do for you, I'll give you five pounds up front since you are low on funds. When you sell out, pay me two hundred dollars apiece and for every five you buy, I'll front you five more until you get on your feet, papi."

Peanut was loving what he was hearing and with the deal he was giving him, he knew he would come up in no time.

"That's a bet." Was all Peanut could say.

"I got five for you right now, where's your car?" Right when he said that he saw Mimi pull up.

"Outside. Just drop them off in the blue Kia right outside."

Los said nothing as she got up. Peanut watched the whole thing go down. He saw how Mimi looked at him crazy as he sat the small duffle bag on the backseat. Peanut waited until he left to make his way over. He paid for his goods and walked out of the restaurant. When he got to the car, Mimi was by herself. He barely knew her but he knew her and her sister was close enough to always be together. He got in as she cranked the car up and drove off.

"I'm sorry about how that went down. It just all happened too fast. Jay was supposed to be here, but I guess he couldn't make it." Peanut explained himself.

"Naw, it's cool," she said back. "Where are you going?"

That question caught him off guard because he didn't know where to take the weed. He couldn't take it to Jay's house because he didn't know where he was, and he really couldn't take it to Big Momma's house. He looked at her and all she did was laugh.

"I thought you were the brains out of y'all two and you ain't even got nowhere to go." She just shook her head and kept driving down New Braunfels Street. She was going to say more but her phone started ringing.

"Hello."

"This is Mr. Smith calling back about the house on Bee Street. May I speak with Ms. Jackson?"

"Yes, this is her," she spoke as she pulled into her hotel. Peanut just looked at her in confusion but didn't say a word. They both just sat there the whole time she was on the phone which seemed like a whole hour. Peanut could tell by the way she talked that she wasn't from the hood, and he was gone find out more about her.

"That was the man about the house. He said it's six hundred fifty dollars a month including water, gas and lights. He said we can meet up tomorrow and sign the contract," she said as she watched Peanut. Peanut paced around the room with a million thoughts running through her head.

"Look, you could keep your little package here until everything gets situated with the house, " she voiced while looking at his small duffle bag. At that moment, he had decided not to hold nothing back from her.

"Do you know what's in that, brah?" He asked her.

"No, but it don't matter."

"Look, if you wanna know what's going on, I'll tell you." He ran the whole story down to her about how they got the weed in the first place. When he finished, he thought she would have a lot of questions, but she didn't. He's gon' start back up, but his phone rang. When he saw it was Erica, he answered it.

"Talk to me, Mami," he said through the phone.

"Hey Papi, I got some people up here that want some weed if you still have some," Erica said.

"Yeah, but they gon' have to wait until I get situated first."

"Okay, just come up her after school."

"Alright, Mami," he said and hung up. "What's up, you wanna kick it with me today? I need to move around to make a couple dollars."

She looked at Peanut and thought about the question. "I'm not tripping, but my sister should be coming back any minute."

"Cool, let's smoke something because my nerves are bad. As they sparked up the blunt, the hotel room door opened and Diamond walked in with some papers in her hand. When he looked, he saw that they were job applications. He passed the blunt to Mimi and stood up. Mimi barely hit the blunt as she explained to her sister what they would be doing today. She agreed as they walked out of the door.

Chapter 6

Jay sat in Bubba D's backyard with Trey, Papa, EJ, and Bubba D. They were all older than Jay and Peanut, so they got stress a little bit better. Jay had asked them to meet there for one reason and one reason only, to put together a stomp down on anybody who don't want to cooperate with them. Peanut had called him a couple of times but he ignored it because wanted to handle the much-needed business. He felt like he needed to contribute something to the hustle, so he figured putting this together would do the job.

"Alright, I called y'all here on some serious business. I know we all tryna get money and me and Peanut got the way. We just need some help," he spoke while giving them eye contact. When he realized he had their full attention, he continued. "We need y'all for the gangsta shit, but we still gon' get money together. If anybody ain't down with the movement then we going to push they ass off the map."

They all nodded their heads in approval.

"I got a hook up on some shit we are gonna need. As a matter of fact, excuse me," Bubba D voiced as he pulled out his phone and stepped towards the back gate. Bubba D was short and stocky and walked bowlegged. He wore an all even haircut with waves and a full beard. He was light skinned with Chinese like eyes and a deep voice. As he talked on the phone, Jay and the others talked about locking down the hood. As soon as he got off the phone, he walked back to where everybody was.

"My homie said he'll hit me up later on with some info on what he can get," Bubba D called.

"Okay if we do it this, we do it my way. If I spot any sign of weakness or disloyalty in any of you, it's over." He made a gun with two fingers to make sure they understood. Jay looked at his phone to read the text message he had just got. Peanut had let him know the details on the house, which made him smile.

"Alright, first thing first, we lock this bitch down always but surely take over every hood in our path," he said as he stood up.

"When do we start?" Trey asked.

"As soon as Peanut hit you up," He stated. "I gotta go handle some business, Bubba D. Get at me as soon as you hear back from ya homie." Jay started walking back up front and spotted his momma's car. That's when he really realized that things had to go right. He needed his own shit He got in and drove off in silence just so he could think. As he turned out of the Carson Homes on Walters Street, he spotted Mimi's blue Kia Rio coming down the street. Before he could even think about turning around, she was already making a U-turn. She caught up to him and he saw Peanut signaling him to pull over. He made it across Walters Bridge and pulled into the McDonalds. Mimi pulled up on the side of him and Peanut got out and started towards his car as Mimi and Diamond went inside McDonald's.

"Damn gangsta, where the fuck you been?" Peanut asked as he gave his homeboy dap.

"Handling some much-needed business that I know we need to get this shit off the ground."

"Oh shit! I gotta hear that shit," he said as he looked at Jay sideways.

"Nothing major just putting us a stomp down team together, but I'll hit you with everything when it's complete. What's up with you blowing my phone up and shit?"

"Earlier, I got with dude Q-Ball hooked us up with?"

"Oh yeah, what's up with that?"

"The nigga broke us off proper."

"What he do for us?"

Peanut explained everything that went down, and Jay's eyes got bigger as he spoke.

"Damn, Mimi down like that?"

"Yeah and I'ma roll with her until I cop my own ride. I'm gonna give you half of the weed to sell so be ready later on tonight," he said as he got out of the car.

At the same time, Mimi and Diamond walked up with food. "We brought you something to eat," Diamond voiced as she passed him his food.

"Y'all over me already," he said as he looked in his bag. They both started laughing.

"You alright. Plus, somebody's gotta feed yo skinny ass," Mimi said as she pulled off.

***

Peanut sat in class contemplating on if he wanted to go apologize to Pastor James. He felt so disrespectful by what he was telling him that weeks had passed without even speaking to him or Big Mama. He pulled out his phone and texted Hazel to let her know what he planned to do. She texted back and told him to meet her after school. He put his phone in his pocket and when he looked towards the door, he saw Erica calling him to the hallway.

As soon as she was going to tell her to wait, the bell rang for them to go to lunch. When he got outside to Erica, he saw her arguing with a group of females.

"What's up, Mami?" He asked Erica as he got close.

"Nothing, just some hating ass bitches mad cause I rejected her ugly ass homeboys," she barked with a thick accent.

"Bitch, fuck you!" One said then tried to swing but Peanut grabbed her.

"Y'all take this shit outside before y'all get jammed up on some bullshit," he said. The girl was so caught up by Peanut grabbing her that she didn't hear what he said.

"Okay, I'll be back since you wanna put hands on me," she said as she walked off.

He didn't pay no mind and Erica walked outside to chill by the basketball court. He was so caught up in his conversation with Erica that he didn't see the group of niggas coming his way. When he heard someone call his name, he looked up and noticed them getting closer.

By the time they reached him, he had already stood up and put Erica behind him.

"What's up blood? You putting your hands on my lil sis?" When he said blood, Peanut knew he was from the Wheatley Courts.

"Look out, gangsta, nobody hit you sister—"

Before he could finish explaining, he felt a fist hit him in his jaw and he stumbled but caught his balance ASAP. Peanut posted up then waited for him to swing. When he did, Peanut ducked and hit homie with a left hook. The hook wasn't powerful, so he threw a flurry of combos that staggered him. Peanut stepped back as the homeboy shook back. A circle had already formed around them, and Peanut had already forgotten about the other three he was with and Erica. When he was about to rush old' boy, he felt the hardest punch he'd ever felt as he hit the ground. When he hit the ground, he felt nothing but feet, so he curled up and covered his face. When the kicks slowed down, he realized people was moving them away. He saw Ray Ray and remembered who he was. Ray Ray helped him up as Erica handed him his backpack. Before he could thank him, all of the teachers came running outside as everybody scattered. Peanut took off so fast that he didn't see where Erica had gone. Before he knew it, he was on New Braunfels. As he was about to get on his phone to call Jay, he heard a horn honk. When he looked back, he saw Erica pulling up behind him. He jumped in and as she drove off, it was silent.

"Are you okay, papi?" She asked as she grabbed the blunt that was in the ashtray.

"Yeah, just drop me off at Jay's house."

She passed him the blunt then looked at him. She saw a look in his eyes she had never seen. When he realized she was glancing his way, he said something.

"Mami, I'm not mad at you. I'll never let no one hurt you, but I must handle my business. I'ma call you in the morning.

"She pulled up to Jay's house then turned off the engine.

"Papi, thank you and be careful, and when do you get at me again, I got a surprise for you," she said as she leaned over then kissed him. "I love you, Papi."

"I love you too," he said as he got out. She drove off knowing what he was going to do, and she knew she would do anything to help him out.

***

"Where the fuck these niggas at?" Peanut asked with his Glock 9 on his lap. Jay was driving around while Trey and Papa sat in the backseat each holding a UZI piece.

"I don't know but when we ran across them, they ass is grass along with whoever they with," Trey said as he looked out of the window. The car was quiet so when Peanut's phone vibrated, everybody heard it. He looked to see who it was and saw that it was Mimi. He answered it.

"What's up, is everything good?" He asked.

"Yeah, I was just calling to let you know that I got you a room so just stop by and get the key, and I want my money back too."

"Okay give me like an hour and I'll be there," he said. Then, hung up the phone. Jay had just pulled in the Hayes store when Peanut yelled out.

"There them niggas go right there!" He pointed across the street at a corner house. Jay pointed across the streets at a corner house. Jay had backed out slowly so wouldn't alarm them. This little mission would test Trey's and Papas' loyalty. Everybody was ready to ride so they had their windows down.

"Hit the block," Papa said. It took no time to come back around. Papa was sitting behind Jay, so he sat in the window while Peanut and Trey hung outside of theirs. Everybody on the porch was so caught up in what they were doing that they didn't see them coming. Trey was the first one to start busting his UZI then Papa and Peanut followed suit. They had turned the house into Swiss cheese before they let up. When Jay was about to drive off, Peanut spotted someone moving and told Jay to hold up as he jumped out. Before the dude could get to the back of the house, he shot him in the leg, and he fell instantly. When he got up on him, he realized that it was the one he beat up at school.

"I hope yo sister be at ya funeral you fucking pussy!" He kicked him then shot him twice in the head. He ran back to the car and told Jay to drop him off.

Chapter 7

He woke up and realized that he was in a hotel room. He reached over and grabbed his phone and saw a lot of missed calls from people who wanted to buy weed. He texted them his address and told them to come get it. Next, he had called Erica. She must have been waiting on his call because she answered on the first ring.

"Papi, I was so worried about you. Are you ok? Where are you at? I'm coming to get you," Erica said though another phone without taking a breath.

"Chill, E. I'm good. I gotta meet with my Big Mama and my pastor for lunch. We can kick it later," He called while laughing.

"Okay, I have to take a shower but call me later because I'ma surprise you later."

"Okay, girl," he said and hung up. Before he could get out of the bed, he heard a knock at the door.

"Who is it?"

"Mimi, open up!" She yelled. When he opened the door, he almost forgot how sexy she was and just stared at her. She had on a sexy red dress with a black leather jacket and some black high heels He didn't realize he was staring until she started panicking.

"Oh, my God! What happened? Why is your lip busted? And why do you have blood splatter on your shirt?" She asked as she stared at him. He hadn't realized that he still had on his clothes. She had grabbed some ice, put it in a towel and placed it on his lips.

"So, what happened last night?"

"Some shit went down, and I had to handle it," He stated as he continued to explain to her what went down. He heard a knock on the door.

"Who is it?" He asked as he got up.

"Red Boy! You good or what?"

"Yeah, hold up," he said and opened the door "Come on."

Mimi sat down on the chair next to the nightstand as she watched him conduct business. At first, she thought that that one person would come and go, but customer after customer kept coming. The whole time she watched him serve, she saw how he conducted himself like a man, and that's when she knew things would move fast. Everybody that came through the door wanted an ounce or better so the money that was on the bed kept piling higher and higher. When people stopped coming, he said nothing to her and let the money be scattered everywhere and went to take a shower. It took Peanut 30 minutes to shower and get dressed so he didn't think that Mimi would still be there. When he walked in, she was sitting on the bed counting money.

"Boy, do you know you just made over two thousand dollars!" She said with a surprised look.

"I know. That's what I was saying when I was getting it," he said as he sat down next to her. "Look, take half of that for the house and keep the rest for yourself."

When he said that it caught Mimi off guard so her head jerked up quick as she stopped sorting out the money.

"What? You act like I just told you to get naked or something."

"Naw, I'm just not use to people just randomly giving me money. This is your second time doing this and I appreciate that," she said as she gave all her attention to the money.

"What's up? Are you ready to drop me off at my Big Mama's house so you can handle your business with the house?"

"Yeah here's twelve hundred dollars," she said as she tucked her half then headed towards the door. Peanut had tucked his money in his pocket and followed her to the car. They got in and before she started up the car, she fired up a Sweet.

"It's about time you upgrade this little ass car," said Peanut as he laughed and scooted the seat back.

"Nigga at least I got one. I ought to make to make yo ass catch the bus."

All he could do was laugh as he grabbed the Sweet. He felt close to her already and knew he could be himself around her. She turned up her Mary J. Blige CD then drive off without saying anything. The whole ride was nothing but them passing blunt and listening to music. Since they wasn't far from Carson Homes, it took them 10 minutes to get Big Mama's house. She pulled up and parked in front then turned the music down.

"Look, Peanut, I know this might sound crazy, but I can't continue to take the money for free."

"Girl—" He tried to say before she cut him off.

"Listen, I'm not saying don't give it to me but just let me earn it."

He sat in the passenger seat trying to figure out what she was really trying to say. "Mimi, just tell me what you want."

"I'm saying let me ride with you and help you make money. I know it's a lot to consider but trust me, we'll come up a lot faster."

Peanut considered it and knew she was right and decided to give her a chance.

"Okay, just let me get this next drop and I'll drop something on you."

She was all smiles as she leaned over and hugged him. When he turned around, he saw a Big Mama standing on the porch. It had been a few weeks since he seen or heard from Big Mama, and it made him smile. He said his goodbyes to

Mimi and went on. As he walked towards Big Mama his phone rang.

"Hello," he said without seeing who it was.

"Are y'all on y'all's way?"

"Yeah, we are getting ready right now," he said.

"Okay," she said back. "And Michael, we're at Outback Steakhouse off Ingram Road."

"Okay," he said and hung up the phone. He hugged his grandma as they got in her car, and they headed to Ingram Road.

***

Pastor James was standing outside with Hazel waiting on his wife so they could meet with Big Mama and Peanut at Outback Steakhouse, when a smoke gray Benz pulled up. He was confused until the passenger window rolled down and he saw a face he knew too well. He walked to the car and got in. When his wife came out and stood next to Hazel, all she could do was shake her head because she knew who it was. As Pastor James got out and walked back to his wife and daughter, he looked at them and said nothing. They got in the car and drove off without saying a word.

"What was that about, James?" Mrs. James said to him as she headed down Ingram Road. He wishes she hadn't asked that because he knew now it would end.

"Nothing we need to talk about right now," He spoke as the conversation died right there.

He pulled into Outback Steakhouse and they walked to the front door. As soon as they got to the door, Hazel spotted Peanut. She was happy to see him since she hardly saw him at school. She had waved them to where they were. As Peanut and Big Mama got closer, she could tell they had made up already by the smile that was on Big Mama's face. All of them gave each other hugs and then walked into the restaurant. They sat down and got settled and ordered their food.

"So, how's school, Michael?" Mrs. James asked.

"It's cool I guess," he said.

"What about basketball?"

"We're winning every game, but I might really start putting more attention into my classwork," he said.

When he said that, it caught Pastor James off guard because of the information he had just received.

"That's very good, Michael," he said. "Look Michael, about last time…"

"I know you was just trying to look out for me, and I'm sorry for blowing up on you," Peanut spoke.

Everybody sat at the table quiet of a couple of seconds before the waitress served them their food. Pastor James was going to say something but decided to let it go, but he made sure to bring it up later on.

Chapter 8

Mimi and Diamond had the house coming along, and while Peanut and Jay were trapping in another spot, she was holding down the Carson Homes. Mimi had just finished bagging up some weed when she was startled by a knock on the door. She had tucked the weed then went to answer the door.

"Who is it?" She yelled on the way to the door.

"It's Ant. Jay sent me by. He said you had some Killa for sale," he said. She looked out the peephole to see if she recognized him. He didn't look familiar. She opened the door anyways since she figured Jay sent him. Ant was tall and skinny with gold in his mouth. She looked him up and down because something was off about him,

"So, you gon' stare or you gone come in and tell me what you want?"

"Let me get an ounce," He stated as he stepped in while reaching in his pocket and pulling out a wad of money. He looked around real quick then turned around outside of the door to wave his homeboy to come in. As soon as she came from the back with the weed, Ant's homeboy stepped through the doors. When she saw the look on their faces, she knew what was about to happen. Before Ant could move, she had already started taking off towards the back. Before she could slam the door shut, Ant kicked it open and it slammed against her, knocking her flat on her back. The other dude yanked her off the floor by her hair and slapped her so hard that blood flew out of her mouth.

"Bring her ass to the front," Ant said. He dragged her to the living room as she kicked and screamed.

"You might as well kill me because whatever you want I ain't given up," she spat.

"Bitch!" That was all he could say as he punched her in her mouth. "You talk when we tell you to!"

"Where's ya boy, Peanut?" Ant asked. "You know at first I thought they was lying when they said the lil nigga was finna open up shop in the hood, which was cool, but the nigga doing too much now. It seems like he is hogging all the money. So, I tell you what we gon' do. We gon' take everything in the crib and make y'all burn off."

Mimi stayed quiet, wondering how Peanut and Jay would react once they found out. When she was finally about to speak, Ant pulled out his gun and slapped her across the face, knocking her out.

***

It seemed like school was going slower and slower so when the bell finally rang, he took his time leaving out of class. When he got outside, he saw Erica waiting outside with an older woman that she resembled.

"Hey Papi, this is my mom, Marisol." He was about to hug her and kiss her until she said that, so he backed up quickly.

"Hi, Mrs. Marisol. I'm Michael."

She laughed and gave him a hug. "Oh, Erica, I like him. Sexy and he's nice. I came to take my daughter to get something to eat. Do you wanna come?" She asked.

"Yeah, only if I'm buying," he said.

When they started walking towards the car, Jay sped up and stopped in front of them.

"Peanut, we got a big problem. Mimi got robbed and beat up bad," Jay said.

Peanut said nothing to Erica and her mom as he hopped in the car. As soon as they sped off, Erica was right behind them. Since Carson Homes was not far, it didn't take that long to get there. When they pulled up, Bubba D, Papa. Trey, EJ were standing outside waiting on him. He hopped out of the car and ran straight in the house without saying anything to his team. When he got in, Diamond was putting ice on Mimi's face. He didn't like what he saw, and it instantly made him angry.

She looked up at him and instantly started apologizing.

"I'm sorry, Peanut. I promise I'll find a way to pay you back. Just please let me and my sister stay," she said as she started crying. He grabbed her hand and pulled her toward him.

"Look, I know this wasn't your fault so you can quit all that crying. This is your house just as much as ours. So, of course you can stay. Somebody ran in your spot and it's gotta be handled. Tell me who done it so I can make sure it won't happen again," He said.

"Some nigga name Ant," she stated while wiping her tears.

He said nothing as he pulled out his gun and walked out of his house. Erica and Marisol were standing outside of the crew as she made eye contact with him. He took off walking down the street and his team followed right behind him with no questions asked. When he got to Ant's house, two niggas was sitting on the porch. They was about to say something until they saw the gun and the redness in Peanuts eyes.

Bubba D and EJ was already beating the living shit out of them before Peanut kicked down the door. Peanut let off two shots and dropped whoever was coming out of the back. They and Papa was shooting at somebody, but it didn't matter because he only wanted Ant. He heard noises coming from the bathrooms and when he was about to open it, a naked bitch came running out. He paid her no mind as his eyes locked on Ant. All he could see was his golds and proceeded to go for them. He turned his gun around and hit him in the mouth instantly, knocking him down. As he fell, Peanut jumped right on him and continued to hit him with the gun.

"Bitch Ass! Nigga! Don't! Ever! Touch! Nothing! Of! Mine!" Peanut said as he kept pounding away. Jay pulled him off of him as he lay there bloodied. Peanut pointed his gun at his head.

"I would kill yo bitch ass, but you live to tell the hood that I'm the head nigga in charge. If I find anybody stepping on my toes, they're dead," he stated as they left.

When he got back in the house, Mimi and Diamond were still in the same spot he left them in.

"Don't worry, girl. Everything good and it won't happen again."

"Thank you," Diamond said. Him and Mimi looked each other in the eye and they both knew he would never let nothing happen to them.

"I'll be back later on. Trey and Papa gone kick it with all for a lil bit," he said as he walked out of the door.

Chapter 9

"I'm telling you the boy looks familiar. I just can't put it with a face," she said.

"Mom, you probably seen him somewhere before and just don't remember," Erica replied.

It had been a couple of days since she had heard from him so she decided to call him. She grabbed her phone and sat on the couch. The three-bedroom house was well maintained. It had the latest furniture that was leather brown, a 72-inch flat screen T.V., plus a whole entertainment system.

Peanuts had answered on the first rings, so she was happy.

"Hey, Papi, are you okay?"

"Yeah, Mami, when can I see you?" He asked.

"How about now my mom is going to my uncle's house," she replied.

"Okay, but I can't stay long because I got to meet someone later."

"Cool, I just want to see you for a little while."

"Okay, I'll be there in about twenty minutes," he said and hung up.

She was so excited that twenty minutes didn't seem like it wasn't enough time. She ran to her room to change clothes and make sure it was clean. When she finished that, she went to go to the kitchen to make some sandwiches for her and Peanut. Her mom had walked up on her right when she was finishing.

"Hey Mami, why two sandwiches?" Marisol said in Spanish.

"Oh yeah, Peanut coming over for a little while, "she said in accent. It was a knock on the door before the conversation could go any further.

"I'll get it," Marisol spoke while walking towards the front door. When she opened it, Peanut was standing there in some navy blue Retro 13s. As he stood there, all he could do was stare.

"Yeah." Was all he could say due to being embarrassed.

"Erica's in the kitchen," she said as she closed the door. She wanted badly to ask him about himself but decided to leave it alone. Before he made it to the kitchen, Erica was rounding the corner with the food and drinks she made for him.

"Hey, Mami, those for us?" He asked her.

"Yeah, you hungry?"

"Hell yeah."

They sat down on the couch next to each other and started eating. Marisol made a hard left to the back, came back and walked right out of the door. Erica loved to be around Peanut, and it killed her not to be around him.

"So, wat happened the other day?" She asked.

"Just some stupid ass niggas tryna play for our spot."

"Well, I'm glad you're okay."

"Look, Mami, I've been wanting to talk to you about something," he voiced while sitting his food down.

"Talk to me, baby."

"I'm about to start doing a little more than wat I've been doing and school is not gone be my number one priority no more," he said.

She sat there quiet trying to figure out what he was getting at.

"I know I might be tripping but I need this money and I want you by my side while I get it."

56

"You know whatever you choose, I got your back, papi." He leaned over and kissed her while pulling her over on top of his lap. She ran her fingers through his waves and stuck her tongue down his throat. Peanut's dick became hard instantly as he put his hand up her shirt. She wasted no time taking off his shirt and started kissing his body slowly. She was excited because she had never done anything like it, but she wanted to do it with him. Peanut noticed her hesitation and looked at her.

"What's up?" He asked.

"Don't be mad but I'm a virgin."

"Don't trip. I got you."

He stood her up and helped her out of her clothes. He was stunned because in the clothes she was sexy but without them she looked like a goddess. She unbuckled his belt as she kissed him. When she got him out of his pants and boxers, her eyes got big because she never saw anything like it.

"Damn Papi, it feels so good!" She moaned out loud. As soon as he sped up and started sucking on her clit, she tried to run, but he locked her legs and went to work.

"Ah! Yes, papi!" Was all she could say. He was so into it that he didn't realize that she came twice already. He stood up and admired her body as she shook from the orgasm he'd just gave her. Peanut lowered his body and was ready to insert his dick. He almost forgot she was a virgin until his dick wouldn't fit. When he finally got in, he slowly stroked until she got used to. She was so tight around him that he didn't want to leave.

"Papi, make love to me," she managed to say during moans. He slowed down more; he didn't know how to make love but he was gone try.

***

Los drove down New Braunfels with 20 pounds of weed in his truck. Peanut and his boys was moving pretty quick and were calling him once every two weeks. He looked back and saw the same smoke gray Charger following him that's been following him for the pass few drops. He was nervous as hell as he pulled up into Johnny's Mexican Restaurant. He never knew why Peanut always chose to meet here, but he instantly felt safe. Maybe it's because they keep straight and his heart slow. He parked and sat in for a couple of minutes before he got out. Right when he go out, he saw Peanut get out of a black 2010 Camry. When he got out, he saw the same female he came up here with everything he came. He nodded to Peanut as they both walked in and sat in their regular spot.

"What's up Los, baby? It looks like you're all scared and shit," Peanut said.

"Naw Papi, I'm good. What you got for me?" He shot back.

"I got four thousand dollars for the whole load," Said Peanut.

"I got twenty pounds now, but I don't have twenty more for the front."

"Naw it's cool. Just get me when I need it most," Peanut said as he studied his face. Los was surprised at how the kid thought because his uncle gave him the same game, and only few people knew that game.

"Okay, for show. I liked the way you think. Anyways, I like that you got yo own ride. I see business is doing good," Los said."

Before he could say something back, the waitress came and sat their food and drinks in front of them.

"Yeah, it's doing good. We just need to expand our net worth."

"Maybe you should try another side of town." Los suggested.

"You know, I might look into that," Peanut said while stuffing his food in his mouth.

"Maybe I can send you to a place, but you gone have to take it." Peanut and Los conversated about the spot then came up with a solution. Los had got up and went through the same thing he did when he was switching money and drug cars. Peanut paid for the food as he waited for his to go tacos. He turned around and saw Los's truck outside. He usually leaves before Peanut goes to his car but is still sitting there, which made Peanut think. He squinted and saw another person in the passenger seat.

Los never came with nobody, and Peanut always told him to never ride alone. He dialed Mimi's number and she picked up instantly.

He couldn't say nothing because she started talking.

"Peanut, I think the dude you always talk to is getting robbed by two dudes," she said.

"Okay, there's an extra gun in the glove compartment. Grab it and follow my lead," he spoke and hung up.

He creeped out of the restaurant sneaky and quiet as possible. When he got outside, he put his hand on his gun right when Mimi got out with hers. They walked casually to the passenger side of Los' truck.

Peanut knocked on the window and then busted it with his gun. He followed through with the heat and slapped old boy in the passenger seat. Mimi opened the back door and pointed her strap at the nigga in the backseat. He pulled his gun out and pistol-whipped him until he was unconscious. He pulled the other one in the backseat and told Mimi to get some rope and tape from the back.

When she came back with the rope and tape, Peanut had got in the back. She handed it to Peanut and he went to work on the two.

"I appreciate y'all's help," he said in a strong accent. "I owe y'all."

"Na, it's cool. Family helps family," Peanut said.

"Cool, you got a down one keep her by your side, Papi."

"Fa sho, wat you gon' do about them?"

"I got some shit for them. It's probably the people that's been following me," he said as he pointed to the smoke gray Charger. He liked Peanut and knew he was gone be a boss one day and he was gone to make sure he was the reason. They both got into their whips and drove off.

Chapter 10

It had been a long time since he had spoken to or even seen her, and when showed up to his house unannounced, it surprised him. He hadn't spoken with her since that day, but he decided to schedule a meeting with her to find out what all she knew. He had been waiting in the food court at SouthPark Mall for 20 minutes when she saw her coming down the escalators.

Karen Brown was still sexy and beautiful as hell to be 38 years old. She was a caramel complexion with hair that went to her shoulders. She stood at 5'6 and weighed 118 pounds with ass and titties out of his world. Karen wore some blue jeans that showed off her curves making her ass look super fat, a regular tight-fitting shirt and some high heels. He could tell she was on duty because he saw her gun and badge on her hip.

Karen had grown up with him and his best friend and would do anything for them. They just so happened to be on the wrong side of the law. She also was their lead Detective on their payroll until things got too out of control. She finally made it to him, and he stood up to greet her.

"Hey, how are you doing Karen? I see you still looking beautiful after all these years," he said while trying to grab her for a hug. She stood back and reached for his hand for a handshake. She was still salty about how he read her after he'd found out about her and Gray.

"I'm doing fine sir, and it's Detective Brown," she said as he sat down. She saw that he looked good as hell and that made her think about Gray. She missed him so much. That's why she always kept an eye on his son.

"I'm sorry I couldn't talk last week. I was busy."

"So, Pastor, how's life treating you? I can tell that talking about God certainly stole your effects," she said sarcastically.

Girl, I'm not here to play your stupid little games. Just tell me about the boy!"

"Well, if you would have been paying attention to him like you always promised, you would know!" She spoke through clenched teeth ready to explode.

"Look, I know I haven't played my part, but now I have my chance."

"Okay, Michael has a case file that's starting to build up from drug dealing, burglary and murder," she said handing him a brown file folder. He opened it up and scanned through it. His mouth fell open because he didn't know Michael was moving so fast and following directly in him and his father's footsteps.

"Damn I didn't know he was moving like this. Don't worry I'll do my best to talk some sense in him.

"James, talk to him more. Maybe you'll get to know him. His birthday is next week, July 24. Make sure you remember," she said as he got up. "And you can keep the file as a copy, I got plenty."

All Pastor James could do was watch her as she walked away. He had to talk to Michael fast, and he knew exactly how to do it.

***

Cesar sat in his office at the back of his newly opened restaurant. He owned a chain of Spanish food restaurants that were doing very well, and Jalisco's just so happened to be his favorite. He had a meeting with a friend from back in the day in a few minutes. He picked up the phone and dialed the front register.

"Hello Maria, I have a friend coming by. Could you set us up in the back?" He asked.

"Sure, no problem," she said and hung up. He poured himself one more drink, because he didn't understand what his meeting was about. He hadn't heard from him in years, and to his understanding, he hated his guts. He downed the rest of his drink and stood up to get himself together. As he walked through the door, he saw the front door open where he'd spotted James come though. He gave a head nod and walked out the back as James followed. He could tell that James had gotten his life together and was somewhat proud of him.

They sat down and just stared at each other in silence. The last time they saw each other, bad shit had happened, so this moment was awkward.

"So, what is the purpose of this meeting, James?" Cesar asked, sounding like the Puerto Rican he was.

"I see you want to cut straight to the chase."

"I just don't have no time for more bullshit. So, tell me what you want so I can go about my business."

As soon as he was about to speak, the waitress came with a pot of coffee and gave them both cups. She had offered them a number, but they denied and said they wouldn't be long.

"I want to talk to you about one of my boys that's starting to get heavy in the streets," James said.

"So, what do you want me to look out for?" Cesar asked to clear his confusion.

"Now, I just know that you supply half of San Antonio, if not all of it. I know this one is deep and getting deeper and I just wanted to know if you know anything about him."

He looked at James and thought but he was old friends with him and Gray. They had helped him come up so when he had to do what he had to do, it hurt him.

"Well, seeing that I'm no longer head of that department anymore so I don't know nothing about nobody kids and if I did, what makes you think I would let yo interfere with my money."

James was hot at how he just handled him so he just stood up and walked off. Before he could get to the door, Cesar called him.

"Oh hey, Pastor James, don't think just because you make the outside look good doesn't mean that the inside is good also. I know about the dealings that you and my nephew have going on. How would the wifey feel if she found out?" Cesar said with a slight smile on his face.

James would've bet his last dime that Cesar always knew about those dealings. All he wanted to know was what Peanut was up to. He started to say something but decided to let it go as he walked out of the restaurant.

Cesar watched as he saw James pull off. He was so caught up in watching James that he didn't even see his nephew walk in.

"Hey uncle, you alright?' He asked, snapping him out of his daze.

"Hey Sabrino, I'm good," he voiced back but still thinking of James. Cesar knew exactly what James was talking about, but he never met the young man his nephew always talked about.

"I just had a talk with a friend that I knew a long time ago, and he was asking about a kid he knew. He said the kid is deep and I got a feeling that he's talking about your new friends.

"And, so, what about me?" Los asked with a confused look on his face.

"I think maybe it's time we have a sit and talk with your new friend about an opposition."

Los was still confused but he knew not to question his uncle. Cesar sat back down and thought about what he would say to the young man that James was so concerned about.

"What's up with you and Big Jay? Y'all look like y'all just got into it," asked Los.

"Naw, just a misunderstanding. Make sure you handle that business." Los left his uncle in deep thought; he didn't know what was about to go down, but he knew he wanted to be a part of it.

Chapter 11

Big Mama was throwing Peanut a birthday party, and everybody was there including, Pastor James and his family. Karen Brown was there also. When Peanut saw Hazel, he walked over to where she was.

"Hey Hazel, how are you doing?" Peanut asked.

"What's up, birthday boy? Are you having fun or what?' she asked.

"Yeah, this is cool, Big Mama and Pastor James came though huh."

"Yeah, you know he always talks about you." Before he could finish his conversation, Erica called him to the front yard. Hazel gave her a stank look as he walked off toward her. It was around 7:00 pm and the party had just started, so people were still coming.

"What's up, E?"

"This same car keeps passing by and yelling out of the window," she said.

Right when she said that a black car bent the corner. This time, they threw bottles instead of yelling. Jay and the rest of the crew had just come from the back when that happened and that pissed them all off. Pastor James and Karen had seen what just went down and started to calm the crew down. Peanut and Jay wasn't trying to hear nothing the pastor or the new chick was trying to say. It took Mimi to calm Peanut down and Pastor James thought about how Karen was the only one who could calm Gray down.

"Michael, let me talk to you for a minute," he said.

Peanut gave him a fucked-up look but he still walked towards the back with him and Karen. Peanut couldn't help but stare at Karen because she was beautiful as hell.

"What's up, Pastor James, who's your friend?' He asked looking at Karen. She saw how handsome Michael was and how he looked just like Gray. She could tell he had his charm by how Hazel, Erica, and Mimi acted around him.

"Hey Michael, I'm Karen I grew up with your daddy and Pastor James," she said while giving him a hug.

"Look Michael, I wanted to talk to you about something," Pastor James spoke, interrupting the hug.

"Okay, shoot."

"Well, I have a friend who's been telling me about some of the things that's been going on in the streets, and your name came up," Pastor James said to him, and he looked at Karen.

"So, what I know a lot of people. I'm a basketball star at my school and of course people are gonna talk about me," Peanut said with a nonchalant attitude.

"Boy ain't nobody talking about no damn basketball," he barked with frustration. "Yo ass is knee deep in the streets with a whole bunch of cases building up. We just tryna warm your ass before it's too late."

Peanuts looked from Pastor James to Karen.

"Look, I appreciate y'all's help but I gots this under control, and if I need y'all's help then we can talk," he said calmly then walked off. Pastor James was so pissed off that he didn't realize that he grabbed him by the arm.

"Boy I'm just tr…….."

Peanut didn't give him time to finish before he snatched his arm back and told him something.

"Nigga if you ever put yo hands on me, you gone need somebody to preach at yo own funeral, Playboy!" He said then walked off. Karen looked at Pastor James like he was stupid. He realized that everybody in the backyard was staring, and he too walked off, feeling stupid.

By the time Peanut went to the front, nobody but Mimi and Diamond was standing in the front of his house.

"What the hell is this nigga doing here?" Peanut asked Mimi as they kept walking.

"I don't know if he knew where we stayed," she said back.

When they got closer, Los stepped out of his truck looking out of place.

"Yo, Papi, I've been tryna reach you all day," said Los.

"How do you know where I stay?"

"I know a lot of things but that's not what's important right now. For some reason, my uncle wants to have a meeting with you and I'm here to pick you up," Los said with a smile.

"Cool but I will drive myself," he stated as him and Mimi got in his car. He lit up a Newport, turned up the Future that was in the deck, then pulled off right behind Los. Before they could get on the freeway, he turned down the music.

"I want you to stay in the car and if I'm not out in thirty minutes to an hour, take off and tell the crew." He explained to Mimi.

"Okay," was all she could say. This was the only time he we had saw Mimi nervous and he didn't blame her because he was nervous himself. It took them 20 long ass minutes to get to his uncle's house. When they pulled up to the gates, Los got on an intercom and the gates opened. They drove to the front door. He looked at the big house and hoped like hell shit turned out good. He pulled his gun out and made sure it was loaded. He looked at Mimi then got out. He followed Los inside and was amazed at how the house looked. When they got the back office and walked inside, an older Puerto Rican man was sitting behind the desk,

"Fellas have a seat," Cesar said and walked to the bar to grab 3 glasses and a bottle of Tequila 1800.

"I'm Cesar, Los' uncle, and you must be Peanut," He greeted and extended his hand. "I've been hearing a lot about you." He looked at him and understood why James was so concerned about them. The kid looked just like his dad, and from the way James tells it, is heading right in his footsteps too.

"So, what's the point of me being in this big ass house when I could be at my party," he said.

"Because I have an opportunity of a lifetime. Seeing that you helped my nephew, and a certain person wants you off the streets, and that person and I don't see eye to eye, I want to help."

"Who the hell could want me off the streets?" Peanut asked with confusion.

"You know him by Pastor James. He came to me about you. Me, him, and your father go way back." Cesar went on to tell about James but leaving a whole bunch of parts out. Los was so confused cause all of this caught both off guard. Cesar paused for a second to pour all three of them drinks. Peanut downed his so quickly that neither one of them saw it go down. He was pissed off at how Pastor James kept tryna be his daddy and run his life.

"So, what is the opportunity you have for me?" Said Peanut.

"Well, consider it my birthday gift to you. I'm willing to up your package if you're willing to up your package. If you're willing to make some money and elevate your game to the next level."

What kind of dumb ass question is that, but I can afford to buy my own weed now."

"Naw, Papi, you misunderstand me when I say next level. I'm willing to give you cocaine if you are up for the challenge," Cesar said while eating.

Peanut thought about how him and Jay and how Jay wouldn't pass up the opportunity. Plus, he knew it would piss off Pastor James.

"Sure, but how much is it gone cost me?" Peanut asked.

"Nothing, first batch is on me. Next batch comes at eighteen fifty a brick, pure fish scale."

Peanut didn't know numbers, but he could tell by the look on Los' face that it was good. He stood up shook Cesar's hand and promised him he wouldn't regret it. He watched Peanut walk off and thought about how his father went out and it pained him. Peanut didn't know what he just got himself in, but he'd just stepped his game up big time.

Chapter 12

Jay, Papa, Bubba D, Trey, EG and Mimi sat in the living room waiting for Peanut to get off of the phone. He was on the phone sealing up the deal that Cesar had offered him the other night on his birthday. He had gathered everybody to let them know about what was about to take place.

"Okay, last night I had a lil ol' meeting with the connect and shit just took a turn for the good." Explained Peanut.

"What do you mean?" Jay asked.

"Cocaine, no more weed. If we gon' takeover might as well do it right."

"Now that's what the fuck I'm talking about boy!" Jay said excitedly.

"Now all we have to do is find different spots for everybody and somebody who know how to cook it then it's a go."

"Got a cousin that could use the job. Plus, he a rider. You can't beat that," said Bubba D.

"Cool, call him up so we can get this show on the road," He spoke then looked at Mimi. "You got this spot under control or what?

"Yeah, I'ma lock this part down," she said with doubt.

Peanut knew she was still shook up about what happened to her a couple of weeks ago. He called Jay and Bubba D to the back to discuss the situation.

"Before we take off to get at these niggas for this new spot, we got make sure shit good here, first." Peanut explained.

"Cool, lets handle up," Bubba D said while pulling out his gun.

"T-Nice the only nigga in the hood who's even doing something," Jay said.

"Well, the nigga either get with the program or get pushed off the map."

Nothing else was said as all three of them walked back to the front and out the door. Even though neither one of them had their guns out, the people that were standing outside could tell that shit was about to get real. T-Nice stayed around the corner on Erwin Street so it was just a minute walk. All T-Nice sold was crack, so at first it wasn't a problem but now the game head just changed. Dope fiends were lined up in front of his door when they hit the block and that fueled their greed even more.

Peanut cut in front of everybody and each one he cut in front of got pissed off and cussed him out. Right when they got to the door, T-Nice opened it.

"What the fuck is all the commotion about?" He yelled when he opened the door. He was surprised to see his lil homies standing at his front door.

"What the fuck y'all want." He asked them as they all smiled at once.

"Ya spot nigga!" Peanut said while putting his gun to his forehead and pushing him inside. They thought he was alone until they got in and saw the other niggas chilling, bagging up crack rocks. Bubba D wasted no time and fired 3 shots at one nigga that jumped of the couch. One hit him in the chest and 2 snapped his head back killing him before he hit the ground.

"Next nigga that moves won't live to see their kids graduate!" Jay said with spit flying out of his mouth.

"Here's the deal, you or yo niggas can't move shit in this neighborhood no more. If you do, y'all won't breathe another piece of this good air," said Peanut to T-Nice.

T-Nice started laughing which made Peanut laugh also. Jay and Bubba D look at Peanut with a confused look. Before T-Nice or anybody could say something, Peanut put a hole in T-Nice's face, splattering blood everywhere. Jay and Bubba D emptied their clips on the other two that were in the house. No word was said as they got up and walked out. All the dope heads was still there waiting to get served and didn't care about shit that just happened.

"Y'all can have every piece of crack in this bitch, but just know, nothing gets brought through this bitch unless it's through me." Said Peanut making sure every one of them got the point.

***

The Heritage Apartments sat right off of Hwy 90 and Babcock Road. The apartments look like nothing was happening but Peanut figured if Los sent them, something had to be shaking. Since Los said that he was gone have to take it, he brought his whole crew including Bubba D's cousin Bay Bay. Papa rode with Peanut, EJ, and Trey rode with Jay. Both cars were full of guns because they didn't know what had happened. Peanut drove inside the apartment and spotted a group of girls then called out, "Hey sexy, let me holla at you."

The one that turned around was so pretty that Peanut's mouth fell open. She was led to the car and the hips swayed. You could tell she had ass.

"What's up, what do you need?" She asked.

"I was gone ask you if y'all was looking to buy some weed," Peanut said lying.

"Naw, we sell weed."

"Cool, well since I'm fresh out how about I buy some from you. By the way, my name is Peanut, what yours?"

"Roxy. Pull over and come in," she said as he gave him a seductive look. Peanut pulled over and told Papa to wait for him. When he got out, the other girls looked at him seductively too. He walked inside and saw that they barely moved in and right there he knew he had a spot. She came from the back with some weed already lit up and a H-E-B bag full. She passed the blunt to him and asked him what he needed.

"Nothing really, I just wanted to chop it up with you alone," he said. She was mad but the nigga was fine as hell, so she let it go. She had never been around a black dude before and wanted to see what it was about.

"I'm out scoping the scene to see how the money is and I just so happen to run across one of the baddest bitches I ever seen. So, I had to stop," he said tryna figure out if he was gone fuck real quick.

"Oh yeah, let me show you what a bad bitch could do," she said as she went for his belt. He said Money and pulled out his dick.

Her mouth dropped opened. "Damn, boy this shit got to be 9 inches. This shit is fat ass fuck," she said while jacking him off. She licked the head then immediately went to work on his dick. The head was so good that he backed up, but she pulled him back. It was so much spit that dripped off his nuts as he continued to suck. She looked up at him and could tell he was enjoying it. When he saw her ways, he knew he was about to bust.

I'm about to cum." He managed to get out. To his surprise, she kept sucking as she put him as deep as he could go. He busted straight down her throat, and she slurped up every drop.

"Damn ma, I like you already. I just might stick around."

"Good cause we need a nigga with big balls around here," she spoke, wiping her lips.

"Oh yeah, what's the problem?" He asked.

"Well, it's some niggas around the way tryna say we can't hustle unless we pay. Trust me it's a lot of money and the niggas don't want nobody hustling." She explained.

"Oh yeah, just point me their way and we can handle this right now."

The crew made their way around to the middle of the apartments and that's when they saw a group of bald-headed Mexicans sitting on the steps. You could tell they were getting money. Just by the way that they carried themselves. He ran it down to his boys on how lil' mama had just put some fire head game down, gave him her spot, and gave all them stew head ass Mexicans up.

They sat down on the stairs across from them just so they could see them. It was jumping so a lot of people were moving around. It was money flowing through this bitch and Peanut had to have it. Every person that looked like a dope fiend stopped and they could tell it was pissing them off. One of the Mexicans finally got the balls to say something.

"What's up, homies. Where y'all from esse?"

"East Side, you got a problem?" EJ said standing up.

"Yeah y'all not allow over here."

"I post where I wanna post. Plus, my lil mama say y'all on some bullshit," Peanut said as he pulled out an all-black 40 Cal. And his crew did the same thing. "As matter of fact, I'm the new nigga in charge and I'm saying y'all can't post up here no more!" Peanut said loudly.

When he said that, about 10 Mexicans pulled out their guns and started firing. Everybody dove to the ground in hopes not to get hit. Peanut was hiding behind a car right next to Jay, and when they looked at each other, they both had a smile on their face. Bullets were flying everywhere so neither one of the crew got to shoot their guns.

When the Mexican finally ran out of bullets, Jay was the first one to jump up and start shooting his twin 9s. The first one he spotted was the one that was talking shit. He shot his way four times and hit him twice in the stomach and when he dropped, he was right on him.

"I see you ain't talking that fly shit now, homes," he said as he shot him one more time in the forehead. He looked up and saw that Papa and EJ were headed to where the rest was and dropping them one by one. Peanut, Trey and Bay Bay were holding down some more that were coming from another way. All you could see was bullets, smoke and bodies dropping. One almost snuck up on Jay, but Peanut realized everything was over with. He counted everybody and made sure his crew was still alive. Satisfied with the results, they all took off running back to where they left Bubba D with the cars running and with the Choppa just in case. They ran past the girl who jumped and told them that they'll be back to turn things.

They pulled off as the police sirens got closer and closer.

Chapter 13

Marisol and Erica had just come from River Center Mall when her nephew, Carlos had hit her up and said he wanted to kick it with them.

"You know it's been minute since we kicked it," he said while laughing.

"Okay, Sobino, meet us at your restaurant," she stated then hung up the phone. She had needed to talk to her older brother anyway so meeting at Jalisco's with her nephew would be the perfect time. Erica's boyfriend had been on her mind ever since she first saw him, and she had to make sure her mind wasn't playing tricks on her. She pulled up in front of her house so Erica could drop the bags off. When she came back to the car, her phone started ringing.

"Hey Papi!" She said, smiling from ear to ear.

"What's up Mami, let's chill," He spoke back. It had been so much going on that he hadn't kicked it with her in a minute.

"Yeah but it's gone have to be later because I'm going to chill with me Familia right now."

"Cool just stop by the crib later and I'll meet you there. He said then hung up. She was excited to meet her cousin, but she was ready to let Peanut get up in her. They had pulled up in Jalisco's parking lot which was crowded as fuck and spotted a parking spot next to Carlos' truck. They jumped out looking sexy as hell. Marisol was wearing a tight-fitting red Michael Kors dress that showed off every curve her body had, especially that ass. Her hair hung past the shoulder, with Cartier frames on her face.

Erica was in some black Levis that showed her ass and a pink Ed Hardy shirt that exposed her titties at the top. Her pink and black Air Max 90s set the whole outfit out. Everybody looked at them as they entered the restaurant. Carlos waved them to where he was sitting at, but Marsol kept going to the back.

"We need to talk," she said to her older brother as she sat down.

"Okay, talk," Cesar said as he stopped filling out his paperwork.

"Erica's boyfriend looks familiar, and it scared me."

"Okay, what is it?"

"It doesn't matter who he is because he's probably nobody, but he looks just like Gray from head to toe. He even movies like him, "Said Marisol.

Cesar sat back because he knew exactly who she was talking about, and he thought the same thing when he saw Peanut for the first time.

"It's nothing. You probably just miss him, that's all." He was trying not to give away nothing. Marisol was in love with Gray but couldn't have him because of so many other females and because the mother of his child had his heart.

"It's been years, it's time for you to let what happens go," he said.

"It was your fault it happened so you should feel guilty too!" She yelled as he got up and walked out and went to the table where they were seated.

"What's up Aunt M? You good?"

"Yeah, I'm good." They sat at the able and caught up on the last past two months. Marisol sat up and listened to Erica talk to Carlos about her boyfriend and the more she listened, the more she thought about Gray.

***

Two male detectives had been watching Jay for the last past couple of days. It seemed like he was doing some illegal activity by all the driving back and forth from one side of town to the next, but they could never get a hold of him doing anything. They were sitting on Drop Zone parking lot when they spotted Jay speeding out of the Carson Homes Housing Projects.

They both looked at each other and knew that he finally got the break that they needed. They sped out of Drop Zone and hit the lights as they went right behind him. They had stopped him right before he got on the expressway. The Detective in the passenger seat whose name was Alverez got out first. Followed by Detective Munoz. They pulled their guns and walked up to the car.

"Let me see your hands!" Detective Munoz yelled. He was a big ugly mean muthafucka with a thick ass mustache. Jay put his hands out the window. They followed procedure and put him in the backseat while they searched the car. It took them 15 minutes to do that, and they came out with 5 ounces of cook up powder. They called the pound to tow the car and they took him to Bexar County Jail. They booked him in and took him straight the investigation room to see what they could get out of him. It seemed like it was hours before they came back to talk to him.

"Y'all might as well go back where the fuck y 'all was cause I ain't saying shit!" said Jay.

"Oh yeah maybe if I read you all the charges you got against you and seeing that you're seventeen years old, you're old enough to go to the big house. Maybe, you'll tell," Detective Munoz said while sitting in front of Jay. Detective Alvarez stayed standing up and before he could add his two cents, the door opened, and Detective Brown poked her head in.

"Alverez… Never mind," she said as she was caught off guard by Michael's friend sitting in the chair. She closed the door and was curious at what he was there for. She decided to listen in and sat behind the glass.

"Failure to identify, unauthorized use of a motor vehicle, speeding, and not to mention the five ounces of crack we found on your possession," Detective Alverez said tossing down a file folder.

"Miss me with all that shit," he stated waving his hand.

"Give me somebody and well see what kind of favors we can get you," Munoz said.

Jay said nothing as they waited for his response.

"Okay, fine. Five to ninety-nine, it's your life not mine. Just know that there are muthafucka in the Big House waiting on light skinned green eyed niggers like you to make their bitches. Take him upstairs," He barked while getting up.

Jay though about it for a minute and realized he wasn't ready to do no time.

"Hold up! I got somebody for you," he said with his head down. Detective Brown's mouth fell open because she couldn't believe what she just heard. She knew exactly who he was about to give up, and she had to get to him before they did.

Chapter 14

Things had been moving fast since they had been moving a whole different product. Now, he saw what Cesar meant when he said a whole new level. They went from $2,500 a week to making $14,000 to $28,000 in one sale. He had parked his car on the side of the church and walked the back way to the house. He threw the backpack he was carrying over the fence and he was right behind it. He was starting to get paranoid lately so he was doing things more secretly. Plus, he hadn't talked to Jay in two days.

He walked through the back door and spotted Diamond in the kitchen.

"What's up lil mama, where's your sister?' he asked while giving her a hug.

"In her room sleep," she said he was about to walk off until she stopped him.

"Peanut, you think I can get some money? I need some shit and its important." She asked.

Peanut didn't hesitate and went into his pocket and peeled off 5 $100 bills. He put his finger to his mouth and walked off to Mimi's room. He checked to see if the door was locked and when it was, he knocked twice then waited until he heard her opening the door. She answered the door in her bra and panties and Peanut's mouth fell open at the sight of her. He knew she was fine, but the woman was stacked with ass and titties, sexy legs, and a slight six pack.

"You gon' stare or tell me what you want?" She said laughing. He walked right past her and flopped down on her bed.

"I need you to help me count this money," he said while dumping the money out on the bed.

"Damn boy that's too much money to be counting. What did you do, rob a bank?" She said.

"Naw I ain't rob no bank, and I know it's a lot of money that's why I need you to help me count it. I don't trust nobody else."

She didn't say nothing else as she turned on the T.V. to BET and lit the blunt that was on the dresser. She was about to sit down until Peanut said something.

"Put some clothes on before we do more than count this money."

She smiled at him and then hesitated before she put on some shorts and a muscle shirt. She was still tired but still counted the money and passed the blunt back and forth. It took them an hour and fifteen minutes to add it all up.

"Damn boy, you must have been pulling overtime because this is two hundred eighty-five thousand dollars," she said as she sat back against the headboard. Counting all that money made their hands hurt and their stomachs empty.

"I have, and it's more where that came from." he said as she sat back.

"Look, shit is starting to get real, and I want you to hold on to this. In case anything happens, you and lil mama will be straight."

She grabbed the money and put it neatly back in the bag. She knew not to say anything because she knew what he meant. Mimi had watch Peanut grow up and become a boss within a year and she as proud at how he ran things.

"Cool, just let me know when you need it."

"I need some food in my stomach," he said smiling. She got up with the bag then left to put it up and made some sandwiches. When she came back, Peanut was laid out cold with his shirt and shoes off. All she could do was smile because he looks damn good laying there. Mimi had loved Peanut for the things that he was doing for them, but at that moment, she realized that somewhere down the line she had fell in love with him. She closed the door, sat the sandwiches down and laid next to him and fell asleep.

****

Karen had been trying to get a hold of Pastor James for two whole days, and it was pissing her off. She just knew that he was ignoring her calls, so she decided to drop by his house. She had just pulled up when she spotted him backing out of his driveway. She pulled up to block him from coming out. Karen stepped out and when he noticed who it was, he got agitated.

"I've been trying to reach you for two days. I'm starting to think you're dodging me," she stated.

He just looked at her frame and started shaking his head because he remembered her as a little girl.

"What do you want, Karen?" He spoke.

"It's Michael. He's in a lot of trouble and we need to find him before the two Detectives do."

"We? I'm done trying to deal with his ass. Now if you will move, I have a service to get to."

"Not if I shoot your tires out," she said while reaching for her gun.

"Okay, okay. Move your car and get in. You can ride with me because I'm not getting in no police car," he said with a fucked up look on his face.

She moved quickly to her car, parked it then got into his passenger seat.

"Now, what kind of trouble has the boy gotten into now?" He asked as he backed up and headed towards his old stomping grounds.

"It's really not him, it's his best friend Jaylon, but he's invoicing him."

He looked at his side and was trying to figure out what she as telling him. When she knew he didn't understand, she started explaining it to him. She had told him everything she had listened in on while Jay was being investigated. She had found out more when she read his file and realized they talked him into snitching for nothing. As Pastor James listened, it pissed him off more and more because Michael was supposed to be smarter than that. He found himself speeding up trying to get to his best friend's son.

They had pulled up to Big Mama's house, hoping he would be there. Before they could make it to the steps, Pastor James noticed that a car stopped on the side of his. When the windows rolled down, all he saw were the barrels of guns. He grabbed Karen and dove straight to the ground. It was so many bullets flying and the sound of bullets ricocheting everywhere. It sent Pastor James back to his old ways. He caught himself reaching for gun he didn't have; Karen was crouched down with a gun in hand but couldn't do nothing because of all the bullets flying.

When the firing stopped, they both got up and ran straight for Big Mama. Pastor James finally realized when she didn't answer and her car wasn't in the driveway that she was gone.

"She must've left for service already. Thanks God," he said as he looked around.

"Oh, my God, what just happened?" She asked.

"That was the same car that came through tripping on Michael's birthday. I'll get Big Mama and she can stay with us," he stated as they walked back to the car. He got on his phone and dial his daughter's number.

"Tell your mom to take Big Mama home with y'all and give her the empty room. Oh yeah, and tell Michael to meet you at Ingram Park Mall."

"For what?" She asked.

"Just do what I say," he said then hung up. He knew it was long shot in getting a hold of Michael and he knew it was gon' be a long day. He texted his wife and told her that he wouldn't make it. Before he could sit his phone down, his daughter was calling him back.

"Yes, baby girl."

"He's not answering his phone, daddy," she spoke.

"Okay baby, thank you," he spoke. "She can't get a hold of him. He must really be laying low."

"I hope so, cause if not, then he's already in jail."

They rode around looking for him and when they realized he was nowhere to be found, they called it a day. It took them no time to get back and go their separate ways.

Chapter 15

Jay had finally got a hold of Peanut and told him that he'd been in jail for the last past week. Peanut and Jay was on the way to Erica's house to get up with her and her friend. Peanut was fucked up with Jay for not hitting him up so he could put up the money for bail. When they got to Erica's house, they parked and got out. Peanut was dressed down from head to toe. He had on some faded fitted blue jean Tru's, and brown Gucci shoes. He had some just got a haircut, so his waves was in order.

Jay was fly himself in some black 511 fitted Levis, a black and green Polo shirt, and some black and green Nike Dunks. They stepped to the door and before Peanut could knock, they was greeted by a yellow bone that looked like a Greek goddess. She was short and petite with green eyes and lips that were juicy as fuck.

"Both you niggas is fine as hell, but which one is Jay?" She asked.

"That would be me and who might you be?" He asked while licking his lips.

"I'm Alicia," she said. "Come in." They walked in and spotted Erica and Marisol in the hallway talking. When she spotted him, she ran and jumped on him and started kissing him.

"Hey, Papi," she said as she got down.

"Hey Mami. How you doing, Ms. Marisol?" He asked.

"I'm fine and it's just Marisol. I'm not that old. My nephew is coming to pick me up. When he comes, let him in," she said then walked to the back. He couldn't help but stare at her ass. Erica caught him and slapped him playfully.

"What you looking at?"

"Now I see where you get all that ass from. If I ever break up with you, I'ma marry your momma. Then, I'ma be ya step daddy," he said while laughing.

"I'll still sneak into your room," Said Erica.

Peanut had just lit up the blunt and passed it to Jay when somebody knocked on the door. Erica jumped up and answered it. When she saw her cousin Carlos standing on the other side, she got happy and told him to come in.

Seeing Los walk through the door caught him off guard because he don't know Erica was related.

"Peanut, what's up, papi?" He voiced, happy to see him,

"What's up, Los? What you doing following me?" He said as he stood up and gave him dap and a hug. Everybody looked surprised including Marisol that had just came from the back.

"I see business doing good. I'm hearing your name from some good people."

"Yeah, it's all good. I need to get at you and the big dawg about some business later on."

"Cool, hit me up and we'll set something up. Hey, you got some more of that shit y'all smoking? I can smell that shit outside," said Los with a big smile. Peanut went in his pocket and pulled out a half ounce of Doe-doe. He wasn't tripping about giving it up because he had more in the car. Marisol was heated because Cesar knew who she was talking about and didn't say shit. They walked out the door. Alicia was all up in Jay's lap, and he could tell shit was about to get freaky.

"How do you know my cousin?" Erica asked still curious.

"We do business together and the reason I'm taking you shopping tomorrow," he stated as he grabbed her and ran to the room. When Alicia saw them leave, she immediately took off Jay's shirt and kissed him from his neck down his body.

"Umm, you smell and taste good," she said as she pulled off his belt. It took her nothing to get his pants and boxers down. When his dick popped out, she eyed it hungrily because of how big it was. Jay felt like he hit the jackpot as she stuffed his fat dick in her mouth. She was trying put the whole thing down her throat, but it was too fat. She came up and bumped his head 3 good times before she went back down.

"Oh, shit, girl!" Was all he could get out. All you heard was slurping, gagging, and moaning. She could ask no more as she got up and took off her clothes. For her to be small, she had a nice ass, and he couldn't wait to hit. She wasted no time and faced her ass towards him and sat on his dick. She moved on his dick slow because it was big and fat. Plus, it kept falling out. When he finally got it in good, she rode his dick like a pro. Her pussy was already creamy and wet, so his dick had juices sliding down it.

"Oh daddy! Yes, I'm coming! I'm coming!" She moaned. Jay started pumping his dick in her, making her come off his dick. He got up and flipped her on her knees and elbows. She cocked her ass in the air inviting him and she regretted it when she felt him plunge his whole dick in at once."

"Fuck! Fuck the shit out of this pussy!"

"This is what you want, huh!" He said as he pounded that ass.

"I'm coming again, daddy. Don't stop!" She moaned.

He sped up because he felt himself about to bust. It didn't take long because he busted what felt like the longest nut of his life. Alicia let out a loud scream because it felt like he grew 2 more inches. He pulled out of her and left her shaking as he went to the bathroom.

***

Mimi had just finished getting rid of the last four and a half and was counting the money. She wasted no time hiding the money in her stash spot. She didn't want to take any risk, especially after she got robbed, so she made her a hiding spot. Mimi went back to the front to wait on her sister when the front door was kicked open.

"Freeze! Get the fuck on the ground!" Detective Munoz yelled while putting an M16 in her face. About six more detectives suited up came in with M16s and searched the place from top to bottom. He put handcuffs on her then sat her on the couch.

"Where is Michael Livingston?" Detective Alverez asked. "We know he stays here?"

"I don't know who the fuck that is, and y'all better have a search warrant to be busting up in my shit." She knew how to play her part and only tell them what they didn't want to hear. Peanut told her that shit was about to get real, so she kept her house clean.

All of the detectives came from the back empty and that pissed Detective Munoz off even more.

"There's nothing here. The whole house is clean. No money or nothing," One officer said.

"What the fuck you mean there's nothing? It got to be something in this peace of shit," Alverez said as he kicked at a plant. All she could do was laugh, which she knew they didn't like.

"The bastard said he would be here and he's certain that it would be drugs too," Munoz said.

"Well, the little bastard lied if you can't tell."

All that shit that was said caught Mimi off guard because somebody had snitched on Peanut. She was quiet, listening to the detectives talk, hoping that name would slip out of one of their mouths.

"Alright, let's clear out." Detective Munoz uncuffed her and stood her up.

"Tell that bastard that I'm coming for him, so be expecting me," he said. She forgot to ask about the warrant, so her mind was on Peanut. They left and she raced straight to her phone and call Peanut.

When he didn't answer, she tried Jay's and he didn't answer neither. She called him one more time and was happy when he picked up.

"What's up Mimi, you alright?" He asked sounding sleepy.

"Hell naw, we just got raided."

That got his attention quick. "I'll be there soon. Wait for me."

Chapter 16

Peanut, Jay, and Bubba D was on the Northeast side of town to scope out Spring Hill Apartments. Their business was growing more and more as they expanded. They started putting some of the other homies in the hood on and giving them spots. On time, Peanut had become the boss he had wanted to be. Soon, he wouldn't even need to touch nothing. Peanut was still salty about somebody dropping a dime on where he stayed. He vowed that he would find out who snitched and handle up.

"Papa said it pumped out here, but shit looks dead to me," Jay said as he passed the Sweet back to Peanut.

"Don't worry, it's gonna pick up and when it does it's mine," Bubba D said. Since Papa and Bubba D scoped the place out, it was rightfully theirs. Peanut pulled out of one of four entrances and pulled up next and parked. They stayed there for nearly an hour before two tall, dark skinned niggas with a mouth full of golds and a head full of dreads came out of one apartment. A navy-blue Nova pulled up right on the side of them. Neither one of them seemed to pay attention to them sitting in the car. They watched the dude in the Nova and one of the dread heads with backpacks and Peanut couldn't believe what just went down.

They just so happened to be sitting right in front of the dope man's house and Peanut couldn't believe his luck. When homie pulled off, he was gone follow him but Bubba D told him to chill and let him and Jay handle it. Before he could say something, they both jumped out and headed to the door. He knocked then stepped back. When they heard the locks turning, they stepped back up close.

When the door opened, he didn't have a chance to say anything. Bubba D jammed the gun in his stomach.

"Do as I say and your intestines won't get blown through ya asshole. Back up slow and act normal." He did and Jay was right behind did, with his twin 9s out, ready for the other one.

"Man, what y'all want?" He asked and they could tell by his accent he was from New Orleans.

"Look, we gon make it easy on you and make you a proposition you can't refuse." They heard movement coming from the back and Jay pointed one of his nines at the one coming from the back.

"Get yo stupid ass next to ya patna," he said as he grabbed and yanked him down.

"Now, you either give yo spot up with no questions or we take it, but either way, it's ours," said Bubba D calmly.

"Now who the fuck you think you is coming up in my shit tryna Debo me? You got to be crazy to think I'm just gon' give up my spot. I'ma give you a proposition you can't refuse. Bounce the fuck up out my shit and I'll tell my boys to let y'all make it," He spoke seriously.

Bubba D laughed out loud because it pissed him off that the nigga was tryna give him an option. He picked his gun up high as he could and slammed it down hard on his mouth.

"You pussy! Ass! Bitch! I tell you what to do!" He said, repeatedly hitting him as hard as he could until he got tired and ol' boy wasn't moving. When Bubba D saw him tryna move his mouth, he shot him in his chest five times and ended his life. Jay didn't say a word as he pumped three bullets in homie's stomach. He fell next to his brother then slowly died.

They shook the house down for whatever money they could find then left out. When they got outside, they saw a whole bunch of niggas with dreads running from the far end of the apartments. They jumped in the car and Peanut peeled out for the apartments. They drove right towards the street and parked in front of a house facing Spring Hill.

"What you doing nigga." asked Jay.

"Nigga we finna go handle up. If we don't, then we don't get the spot fool." He spat back.

They said nothing as they loaded their guns back up and grabbed extra clips. Peanut put his 40 Cal down his pants as he jumped out and grabbed the Uzi in the trunk. They walked back to the apartment and saw the same niggas looking around trying to find whoever did their homies. As soon as they spotted Peanut, Jay, and Bubba D, they knew they were out of place.

Before they could even reach for their guns, Peanut pulled the trigger on the UZI and let loose on whoever was standing in the way. Jay looked at Peanut and saw pure killer. As they got closer, bullets started zipping past them and they all hid behind cars that were lined up.

"Circle around the buildings and hit em' up from the back," Said Peanut. They didn't realize that it would be so many. If they did, they would have brought the rest of the crew. He went around one building and Jay and Bubba D went around the other. The gunfire hadn't stopped until Peanut let the UZI go on the two that was hiding behind a car. Before they realized what was happening, blood was splattered on the car. Jay and Bubba D was going to work on whoever stood in the way as they were getting closer. Peanut's UZI was empty when a dread head snuck up behind him. The dread head pulled his trigga but his heart was beating. He didn't even notice Jay and Bubba Do walk up on him.

"Damn homie, we almost bit off more than we could chew, but it's done," Jay said, snapping Peanut back to reality where the car was parked.

***

After the little incident earlier, Peanut decided to chill for the rest of the night. He sat in his car in front of the house with Mimi and Diamond smoking a Sweet. He told them about everything that went down in Spring Hill, and even though they was all laughing, they were scared, especially Mimi.

"Your ass is doing too much; you better sit down somewhere and find that snitch," said Mimi.

"I'm working on that right now and whoever did it, feel sorry for them," he said. As he hit the Sweet then passed it back to Diamond. "Maybe after that I might call it quits."

Mimi looked at him with a surprised look because she wondered how it would be with him around all the time. She wanted to tell him now she felt but decided not to. He cranked up the car and pulled off.

"Where are we going? To get something to eat cause I'm hungry," said Mimi.

"Yeah," he said.

"Wait, you need to put the gun up," Diamond said as she threw out the doobie.

He did not hesitate by stopping to put his gun up. He was gonna put the weed up too but decided to keep it. He figured since they were only going to McDonalds, it was okay.

He got back in and sped out of the Carson Homes. It was quiet and he noticed Mimi looking at him while he was driving. He saw her look at him like that every time he was around, and he knew the look too well. He knew she liked him and he damn sure was feeling her, but for some reason he couldn't let her know. Peanut pulled in McDonald's parking lot, and he didn't even notice the two detectives parked there too. Mimi got out and went inside and ordered their food. Peanut rolled a Sweet while waiting, even though it wasn't long.

Mimi came back out with the food. He lit the blunt and sped off. The detectives got behind them and wait until he passed a light. Then, pulled him over. Peanut looked in his review and cursed. Then, pulled over.

Detective Munoz and Alverez stepped out as Munoz walked to the car's side. When Mimi saw that it was them, she told him.

"What's up, officers?" He said as he rolled down his windows.

"I finally got yo black ass. Get out so I can search yo ass." Peanut was glad he left the gun but had ounce of weed in his pocket and whole pound in the trunk.

"Look, I'm not going to even waste y'all's time. I got a whole bunch of weed on me."

"Good. Yo ass is going to jail," Detective Munoz said as he arrested him and put him in the backseat of his car.

Chapter 17

When Jay had got wind of Peanut going to jail, he felt bad because he knew it was his fault. He knew he fucked up but Peanut didn't really care about him being in jail. He hated the way people gave him all the respect and loyalty like did all this shit by himself. He was really pissed off about Peanut never taking him to meet the connect even though they saw the same money equally. Jay was on his way to his house from The Heritage Apartments to meet with everybody.

Things was about to change for Jay. For one, Peanut had to give him the connect, and two: he was in charge so now he would get the loyalty and respect he deserved. He smiled at the thought of him being in charge and now shit was about to change. It took him no time to get to the house and when he got there, everybody was there, including all of the new members. Everybody went to the backyard and circled up like usual.

"As y'all know the homie got knocked, but that don't put shit on pause," said Jay

"So, how we gone eat?" said Bay Bay.

"Don't worry about that. I got everything under control, let me handle things. I'll go talk to the homie and see what's up."

"Why are we just sitting here? Let's go bail the homie out!" Papa yelled.

"Because he don't have one," said Mimi.

Everybody was quiet when she said that which pissed her off. She looked at each one of the trying to figure out who put the laws on her a baby. She wanted to cry but she had to stay strong for Peanut.

"We stay doing the same shit, because I know the streets talking. Let niggas know ain't shit changed cause Peanut is locked up."

Everybody nodded their head in unison letting him know everything was understood. Mimi wasn't the only one fucked up about their new situation. Bubba D was also. He nodded his head at Mimi and they both knew what it was about. He knew that Mimi knew the connect and a had to get to him before Jay did.

***

It took Peanut two whole days to get processed and housed. Since it was his first time in jail and his crime wasn't violent, they housed him in the Annex on the 3rd floor. When he walked in, all eyes was on him. Niggas either knew who he was or heard of him and didn't want to try him. He put his bedroll on his bed and went straight to the rec yard for some air. As soon as he hit the door, he recognized his high school enemy, Chris.

When Chris started walking towards him, he shook his head because he didn't feel like fighting.

"Well, well, well, if it ain't Mr. Basketball. What you do, snatch an old lady purse?" Said Chis and he made the whole rec yard break into laughter. When everybody started laughing, he knew Chris had the pod on lock.

"Watch ya mouth, homie," said Peanut. Chris knew about the shit Peanut had going on and didn't want any problems, so he shut his mouth. Chris left the rec yard to get on the phone. By the time he made it to the phone, a female guard was standing at the door yelling. She was fine as hell. Even though she was tall and slim, her body was still banging. She could have been a model because she was pretty as hell and not to mention, she was white.

"Yah, what's up C.O.?" asked Peanut as they stepped in the hallway.

"Carlos sent me up here to make sure everything is all good," she said eyeing Peanut her damn self. Damn, he's sexy she said to herself. Peanut couldn't help but smile because Los was showing him mad love.

"Tell him to hit my homegirl Mimi up and treat her like family."

"Alright and if you need anything, let me know and I mean anything," she said as she licked her lips at him. "Now, turn around and let me search you to make it look good."

He turned around and she started patting him down. As she patted him down, she made sure she ran her hand across his dick.

"Nice," she said as she finished and walked away. Peanut made a reminder to and get at her on a different tip. He walked back in and went straight to the phone and called Mimi collect. He was happy when she answered on the first ring.

"Talk to me, lil mama?" He spoke. "What's going on out there without me?"

"Everything alright for right now, but in about a couple of days, shit is gone slow down."

"Well, when you come up here, I'ma holla at you about some stuff. So, make sure you come.

"Okay, you good in there or what?" She asked.

"Yeah, just make sure you and lil sis is good out there." All she could do was smile because he always made sure they were good.

"Thanks to you we are always good. It's only been two days and I'm missing you like crazy," she said, wanting to cry.

"I know, I'll be back soon. I told you that some shit like this would happen so be strong cause I'ma need you while I'm here. Everything I taught you, you need to put in action because without you, shit gone fall apart. You sat back and watched me build the house and now it's time for you to maintain it." He explained.

She knew what he meant, and she promised him she had it all under control before they hung up. He wasn't off the phone for a hot second before he was called for a Detective follow up. He was pissed because he don't want to talk to no damn police. He tried to refuse but couldn't and made his way out of the door. When he got in the hallway, he realized he didn't know where to go.

"What you are, police too? Well, I don't got shit to tell you," he said as he started for the door.

"What? I'm not here for none of that. I'm here to enlighten you in your situation and let you know who I am."

He stared her up and down because now that he knew she was the law, he had to hear her story.

"Well, my name is Karen Brown. Me, James, and your daddy have been best friends since birth. They ended up running the streets and I became a Detective and a deduction on their payroll. I was in love with your daddy, and he got killed. I promised to look out for you along with James when he died. I went my separate ways and that's why you don't know me," she said.

Peanut was fucked up by what she was saying and was at loss of words.

"About a week and a half ago, I stumbled across an investigation and was surprised at what I heard. The crazy thing about it is the bastard gave your name with no remorse. When I walked in, he didn't even notice me from your party, so I walked back out and sat behind the glass. So, here it goes. I know who snitched on you and who killed your father," she said as she just looked at Peanut." I'm gon' get a hold of your father's old lawyer. He won't charge much, but I assume you can pay whatever he's offering. Now when I give you these names, you promise me that you're done with the streets."

He had already planned on taking a break, so it was no problem with telling her what she wanted to hear.

"Yeah, whenever I handle my business, it's a wrap," he said as he braced himself for the names.

"Okay, the person who killed your father is Pastor James and the one who snitched on you is your best friend, Jaylon."

Both names knocked all of the wind out of him because his daddy's best friend killed him and his best friend snitched and on him. She went on to tell him Pastor James killed Gray because of envy, and was assuming that was why Jay snitched on him.

All Peanut had on his mind as he left was revenge. He thanked her and said he would make good on his promise once Pastor James and Jay bled every drop out of their bodies.

Chapter 18

She had been waiting to see Peanut for the last past hour and was getting irritated. She got pissed off when she got to the front desk, and an officer tried to throw Peanut under the bus just to holla. Now she is waiting for him to show up and it seems like that was taking forever. She made sure she looked at her best so niggas and bitches would know how Peanut did it. The way niggas was breaking their necks to look at her she knew she looked good.

When Peanut turned the corner and sat down, she almost cried.

"Don't start that shit." Was the first thing he said when he picked up the phone.

"I'm not, I'm just happy to see you. I miss you," she said with a smile. She looked at him and even in his orange Bexar County Jail uniform he still looked good, and like a boss.

"I miss you too, but I'm not crying."

"What are they going to do with you?" She asked.

"I don't know. My daddy's friend came to see me. She said she's going to contact his old lawyer so we can have some bread on deck." He explained.

"So, what you want me to give the connect to Jay?"

By the mention of Jay's name his heart started beating fast as he felt his blood rushing through his veins. She saw the way his jaws clenched and was going to ask him what was wrong but decided to let him tell her.

"Naw, don't give that nigga shit. As a matter of fact, I don't want you around him."

"What's wrong? I thought y'all was tight."

"Remember my dad's friend? Well, she a detective, and she told me he was the one who gave up my name." He explained. "That's just half of what she told me. She said Pastor James was the one who murked my old man on some hating shit and probably that was the reason Jay gave me up."

"I would ask you what you're gonna do about it but I already know."

"I need you to run shit while I'm down.

"But what about Jay?" Asked Mimi."

"Don't worry about him. Just talk to the crew and let them know I said that you are in charge now. I already got word back to Los to treat you like family so he should be hitting you up later on."

"Okay, I'ma do my part just make sure you stay out of trouble so you can come home," she said then decided to shoot a slug his way. "But don't worry, I'ma keep home warm and ready for you so when you come home and lay in it comfortably."

He smiled because he caught the slug then decided to shoot one back. "You bet not let anybody lay in my home. I'm crazy about my shit."

She smiled and didn't want to play games anymore.

"I love you daddy, and when you get out, I'll show you what you were missing. I have been down with you since day one when we both didn't have shit. I'm not going nowhere so be cool while I work on getting you home," she spoke seriously.

"I know you've been down since day one. You my ride or die. That's why I need you—"

Before he could finish, the C.O. said his time was up. She got up as he said goodbye. She turned around and she knew he was staring at her ass. She was about to walk off when he banged on the glass.

"I love you too, Mama, and when I get out, I'ma tax that ass!"

"It might be too much for you," she said while she shook her ass cheeks quickly.

She blew a kiss then went their separate ways.

***

Mimi had just got off the phone with Bubba D saying she needed to go talk to him. She was gone let Peanut know he could count on her in any situation and would be the boss bitch he needed by his side, and not no little girl. When she pulled up at Bay Season W.W. White, she spotted Bubba D's ride then parked next to it. She thought he would be inside, but he was in his car rolling up a Sweet. He waved her over to his car and she grabbed her shit and jumped in. He finished rolling the sweet then passed it to her to light it.

She hit then let the smoke settle on the brain as he prepared to tell him the new plan.

"Wat's up with the homie, Peanut?" He asked while grabbing the blunt.

"I just came from up there and he just threw a curve ball, striking Jay out." She explained.

"Wat you mean? What did you tell him?"

"Nothing, it's what he told me."

"Shit, don't leave me in the blind," he said anxiously waiting to hear more. For the last few weeks, he felt that Jay had been acting weird but didn't really pay it no mind. And now he was about to see why.

"Peanut said he's the one who snitched on him. Plus, that bitch ass Pastor of his killed his pops. You've known Peanut longer than me so you can only imagine what he's going to do," she voiced.

He was shocked and mad at the same time. Jay and Peanut had been best friends since they were 10 years old. He couldn't believe his ears.

"Why? I mean they ate together and always split everything down the middle."

"Envy. He was the one who made shit happen. He felt like y'all had more respect for Peanut than him. And I'm guessing because the other person who knows the connect is me and not him."

That caught him off guard because he didn't know she was that deep in the game. Now, he understood the curve ball that had struck Jay out.

"Let me guess, you're the curve ball that just struck Jay out?"

She just nodded her head as she inhaled the smoke.

"I know Jay is not going to like it and I'm not sure about the rest. Peanut told me to tell you to let them know that I'm top dog."

He liked what he was hearing because he damn sure wasn't riding with no snitch.

"Cool, let me handle the crew, which I'm sure gonna be okay once they find out about Jay shit. They might off him."

"Naw, let the Peanut handle that part. Look, I'ma leave it the way he left it. We all eat equally. No more less, no more."

"I like that."

She said nothing as she got out of his ride. He couldn't help but stare at that ass and didn't understand why Peanut wasn't fucking.

"Hey, Mimi!" He yelled.

"What?"

"When you gone let me handle up on ya?"

"Boy, this is all Peanut's." she said then go into the whip.

He smiled then got in his whip. He smiled cause Peanut had her on lock and wasn't even fucking.

Her phone rang as soon as she pulled off and when she saw an unknown number pop up, she hesitated but still picked up.

"Hello," she said through the phone.

"Hey Mimi, this is Los, Peanut's friend. He told me to hit up," he said loudly in his accent. She was nervous because she didn't know what to say. She had seen and heard Peanut conduct business all the time, so she played his role.

"Yeah, but can we meet in a couple of days so I can get shit situated on my end."

"Sure Mami, let me know when you're ready."

"Okay," was all she said then she hung up.

Chapter 19

Marisol didn't know what she had planned to do so it was a long shot when she had gone to see Peanut. She had to clear her mind and see if he was related to Gray any kind of way. It took her no time getting up there to see him. When he saw her, he kept looking for Erica, but she was nowhere around.

What's up, Marisol? Where's E at?" He was confused because she was there by herself.

"She's at home and she wants to come but I need to talk to you about something."

"Okay, shoot, but don't be tryna holla at me on the cool. Just because you look like a sexier version of E doesn't mean I'ma fall for it or I just might "He smiled jokingly.

She laughed because he even had his charm and it scared her. "No, I'm too much for you anyways, Papi. I need to know who your papa is because you remind me of someone I knew a long time ago," she said.

"My daddy's name is Gray, but I don't think you know him."

She started crying instantly because she knew the minute that she saw him that he was Gray's son.

"I knew it from the moment I saw you. You look, walk, and talk just like him." She cried.

"How do you know my pops?" But it quickly hit him when he remembered Los being her nephew.

"I was in love with him, and he helped my brother build one of the biggest empires in Texas. It all got taken away from me because of that puto, James."

"I know and best believe I'm gone get at him when I get a chance."

"You're following in your Papa's footsteps, but make sure you watch who you surround yourself around. Gray was on top of the world. He had money, women, cars, houses and all the respect in the world. He wanted to get out and bring James with him but James wasn't ready because he didn't have what Gray had. He asked Gray to leave him the connect and Gray said no. From there, it was pure hate up until he killed him." She explained.

"I know I was in the backseat when it all happened."

"I'm sorry about all this. Do your time and come home. Take back what was your papa's to start with. Remember it's more than revenge it's payback," she said as she got up and left. On the way back to the tank, he had a lot on his mind and didn't want to be bothered with it. He walked straight to his bunk with intentions of laying down until someone bumped into him.

"Watch where you walking, dawg! These other muthafuckas might fear yo ass but not me!"

The nigga was bigger than Peanut, but he was far from scared. Peanut looked around and saw that everybody was looking. He looked at the guard and when he gave him the okay, he cocked back and hit him as hard as he could. Peanut knew not to give him no kind of time to regain his balance. He threw a bunch of punches that landed everywhere. The nigga fell flat on his back as Peanut jumped on top of him and started pounding him in his face.

"Okay, that's enough!" The guard yelled when he saw blood all over Peanut's uniform.

An old school cat pulled him off of the dude then took him to the rec yard. "Boy you got some gangsta in you but your wild. Let me teach you something and you will be successful in yo street career."

"What do you mean? I'm a half a million dollar a nigga in a year damn successful!"

"I know but I can elevate your game. Meet me out here at 7:00 am. We start with a workout," he said then walked off. Peanut said nothing. All he wanted to do was take a nap.

***

Jay sat on the back porch smoking a blunt by himself. Peanut had been locked up for nearly three weeks and shit was starting to get real. He tried to see Peanut but wasn't able to due to him being on his paperwork. He didn't know what he was gone do about more work because every spot they had was almost out. Jay reached for his gun because he saw movement out of corner of his eye. Bubba D jumped at the sight of the gun.

"Damn nigga, you that nervous to where you gotta pull ya strap on ya homie!" Bubba D said with his hands up.

Naw, it just so much shit been going on. What up gangsta, you good?" He asked while putting his gun up.

"Came to talk to you about some shit."

"Shoot."

"Have you talked to the homie, Peanut?"

"Naw, why?" Asked Jay as he looked at him confused.

"Well, I talked to Mimi and she said he gave her the connect. He said everything goes through her and shit stays the same," Said Bubba D.

As soon as Jay heard that, he turned red as fuck. "You mean to tell me he gave the connect to that bitch and not me! Nigga we been though everything together. We started this shit together!" He yelled as spit flew out his mouth.

Bubba D could tell he was mad because he was on the verge of tears. I know this fucking snitch ass pussy ain't tripping. He wanted to say but kept it to himself.

"He said the connect knew her and only preferred to deal with people he knew. I mean shit still gone be the same so what you trippin for?"

"I'm supposed to second in command, but he put that bitch above me. Ya know it's cool, I ain't tripping because when he realize she ain't got the balls to run shit, he'll call me." he stated while lighting a Newport to calm his nerves.

"Let's just roll with it and see where this takes us." He told Jay then walked off.

Jay was still hot and didn't like what had just happened. He needs to get close to her to meet the connect so he started to come up with a plan.

Chapter 20

Mimi was on the way to meet up with Los and was nervous as hell. This would be her first time dealing with Los and didn't know what to expect. Peanut had to bring one hundred eighty-five thousand dollars for ten bricks and he would give them another ten bricks. He had coached her on their last visit on what to say. Since they had started dealing with coke, Peanut wanted to switch up their meeting spot.

She was meeting Los at one of his spots on the northside, down the street from SeaWorld. It seemed like it took her forever to find the house and when she did , she waited for a little bit. She wanted to bring Bubba D, but Peanut told her to go alone. She checked her purse to make sure her .25 was in it, grabbed the backpack in the backseat then got out.

When she made it to the door, she didn't have to knock as a beautiful blonde-haired blue eyed white girl opened the door.

"He's in the back room waiting on you," she said.

Mimi said nothing back as she found her way to where Los was at. He was sitting next to someone who looked familiar to her.

"Hey Mami, sit down, you smoke?' He asked.

"Yeah, but I'm good," she said white still looking at the other dude as he stared at her.

"I see Peanut taught you well. Talk to me,"

"I got enough for ten bricks, but to my understanding, I'm to get twenty. Before we make our deal, I expect you to treat me as you would treat Peanut. I expect the same deal. No more, no less and I only deal with you and next time, no company.

He shook his head because what she was asking for a was more than understandable.

"True. You're correct about what your here to pick up." He snapped his fingers and another girl came out. This time she was chocolate and beautiful as hell. She came out with four black duffle bags, sat them down, then walked off.

"I can meet your accommodation you've just requested, but you have to meet my uncle," he said back. She was gone say something back, but she was at a loss of words, when she realized who was sitting in front of her. He smiled because he was waiting on her to figure out who he was.

"Cool, here's your money." She gave Los the backpack and he sat it down. She grabbed two bags as she hurried up and made her way to the car. She couldn't believe who she saw in the house and didn't understand why he was there but she didn't want to be around him.

"I'll tell Peanut you did good and would only like to deal with you," he said.

"Okay, just make sure you're not with that nigga in there again or you won't see my money again," she said then drove off. She quickly picked up her phone and called Bubba D.

"Yo! Talk to me," he spoke through the phone.

"Hey, we good. Tell everybody to meet me at the spot," she said back.

"That's what I'm talking about. By the time you make it, everybody will be here. Just make sure you're careful."

They said nothing else as he hung up so she could focus on driving. She had 20 bricks in her trunk, so she had to be aware of surroundings. Peanut said he was getting them at $18,500 apiece and was selling them to his boys for $20,500. Everybody else was getting them at $24,000 apiece. He was selling his *zones* at $600 by powder and $350 by hard. And anything less than that was no good.

She had to remember those numbers so things would go smoothly. Only ten bricks was to go to the homies and ten was to be split with her and Jay. He wanted shit to stay the same with Jay so shit wouldn't be suspicious. Before she knew it, she was pulling up at her crib as she noticed all the cars parked out front.

She called Diamond to help her with the bags as they took them to the back.

"Jay, let me talk to you," she said as she headed straight to the back.

"What up girl, talk to me," he said playing it cool.

"I believe five of these go to you. Just because Peanut locked up don't mean shit gone change."

"Cool."

She wanted to dismiss his ass, but knew she had to keep his trust. "You call all the shots and I distribute the work. As a matter of fact, Peanut told me to tell you about Woodlawn Apartments."

"Oh yeah, I'ma go check those out something this week."

They finished talking and he grabbed his bricks and left. She gave the ten to the crew and got $250,000. So far shit was going good and she hoped to keep it that way.

***

Jay had pulled up to the front of Erica's house with the hopes of getting in contact with Carlos. He sat in front for a minute trying to figure out how he was going to get his information. He jumped out and decided to just go with the flow. He knocked on the door and Marisol answered the door looking sexy as hell. She had on a black muscle T-Shirt that was tight-fitted to her body so she didn't wear no bra. She had on some small pajama shorts and her long curly hair was wet like she'd just got out of the shower.

"Erica and her friend is not here, Papi." she voiced. He was staring and knew it and started licking his lips to let her know. She saw him lick his lips and started smiling.

"I'm not here for neither one of them," He spoke, knowing she couldn't resist him. He knew he would use her to get Carlos' number.

"Well, what do you want?"

"I wanna come in and smoke, but I see you busy."

"Come in."

They looked at each other as he walked in, and they both knew what was about to go down. He sat down and quickly pulled the blunt from the back of his ear and lit it.

She sat next to him and as close as possible. "So, what made you wanna come smoke with me?" she asked and grabbed the blunt.

"Shit, why not come chill with something so sexy?"

"You better watch it. I'm too old for you."

"What! I might be young, but I'm equipped!" He said boasting. They smoked a couple of Sweets back and forth until Marisol came out of her shorts and muscle shirt. She had no panties and bra on, and Jay smiled. He went to work on her titties ASAP as he dug his finger in her fat pussy.

"Oh yes, Papi!" She moaned as he sucked her titties. He kissed his way down to the clean shaved pussy. He sucked on her clit at first then started sucking on her whole pussy.

"Fuck yeah, suck my pussy. Oh! Oh! Oh! I'm coming, Papi. I'm co…" She yelled as she tried to run.

"Damn girl, you even taste good."

She sat there for a minute trying to regain herself from a nut she'd been waiting on for a long time.

"My turn now, Papi." She made him stand up as she stripped him out of his clothes. His dick popped out and she almost ran at the size of it. "Oh, I'm gone have a lot of fun with this." She put her mouth on the tip and swirled her tongue around it as she jacked him off. She opened her mouth wide and engulfed as much of his dick as possible.

"Oh shit, girl eat that dick, Mami. I got something for that ass when you done!"

She soaked his dick with saliva as she gave the best dick sucking of his life.

He picked her up and she wrapped her legs around the waist.

"Don't hurt me with that thing. It's been a minute," she said. He didn't pay her no mind as he slowly put his meat in her tight pussy.

"Damn, girl you tight as fuck." She couldn't say nothing because her face was in his neck as she tried not to scream. He said fuck it and bounced her up and down his dick.

"Ahhh! It's too much fuck!" She screamed and tried to go down, but he held her tight. He continued to fuck her as she screamed...

"I'm com... coming, Papi! Yes, I'm coming!"

He laid her down and she rolled over on all fours. He entered her pussy. He pulled her hair and smacked her ass as he dug deep as he could.

"I'ma making this pussy mine. Who pussy is it?"

"Yours! Papi! Yours!"

He long stroked her as she felt her pussy tighten around his dick and he knew she was about to come. She came again because his dick was good.

"My turn," she said as she moved from his dick and laid him on his back. She hovered over his dick in reverse cowgirl and could only go down halfway. She twirled her ass in circles and made her pussy twerk on his fat dick.

"Oh yes. You got a big black fat dick!"

"Umm!" was all he could get out because he couldn't believe how good this woman's pussy was and she was working it too. He felt himself about to come and so did she because she went in overtime and bounced up and down all the way. They went thrust for thrust as he exploded in her.

Chapter 21

The whole crew had wanted to see what was up with Woodlawn Apartments off of Fredericksburg Road. Jay still didn't have the connect, but still had money to make and shit to takeover. He had gone to Marisol and laid a mean dick game down in hopes to get Los's number out of her. He didn't know that Los was damn near the middleman and he had to get to his uncle.

The apartments was jumping. From hoes, niggas, money, cars. You name it, and it was only 10:00 am. They had sat on some random steps in the middle of the apartments in hopes to come across something. All eyes were on them because nobody knew who they were, and Jay loved every minute of it.

"What's up baby, you got some work?" A lady asked Bay Bay as he came out of an apartment and walked down the stairs.

"Yeah, what do you need?" He said back.

"I need a sixty and do me right and I'll be back, and bring y'all some money," she said. He broke her off with four $20 rocks and he saw how happy she was. He knew she would be back because he cooked all their work. He knew it was a drop.

"Y'all gon' be right here when I get back?" She asked.

"Yeah, but take my number so you can call," said Bay Bay as he rattled of his name and number. She took off not wanting anything else.

"Shit might as well make some money while we out here. This might be the easiest job we've had," said Jay as he pulled his pistol out and sat it on the stairs next to him.

"This might be the funnest job we had. Look at all of these hoes out here," said Bubba D. It was so many bad hoes out there that it had to be a ratio to every three niggas it was five bitches. Fifteen minutes hadn't even passed by and ol' girl that had just copped some work had come back. Everybody knew she was high as a kite, but everybody was paying attention to the bad ass chocolate female standing next to her. Lil mama was 5'5 and weighed 125. She hardly had titties but her slim waist made her ass look fat as hell. Plus, her hips stuck out. She was dressed in some tight orange shorts that showed off her sexy thighs and a white shirt that showed her tight stomach. Her hair went to her shoulder and he almond-like eyes showed honey brown.

"Bay Bay, this my niece, Trina. She tryna get some of what you got," she said. Everybody looked back at the fine one with a surprised look on their face.

"Y'all can get that look off y'all face. I don't smoke that shit. I'm tryna cop a four and a half," she spoke.

"I got you but you gotta follow me to my car," said Bay Bay.

"Cool, which way."

Bay Bay took off and she followed right behind him. Everybody was looking at her as she jiggled. They made it to his car and they both jumped in. She was checking him out and was liking what she was seeing, especially his thug appeal.

"What do you want, hard or soft?" He asked.

"Hard, I can't cook this shit."

He laughed and pulled a 4 and a half out of a lil nap sack he had and handed to her.

"Give me twenty-eight hundred since it is for you, but for everybody else it's thirty-five hundred."

"Damn that love right there, but why?"

"Because I like money. Plus you look good and you like getting money. I respect that," he said while all she could do was nod in agreement.

"You know y'all got some nuts coming out here."

"Why?"

"Because these niggas that run the apartments don't let nobody that ain't from here hustle out here."

"Well, we do what we want to do and if you want to make money, you might as well jump on the money train."

"Cool, I like the sound of that, but just know that y'all better be ready for whatever is coming," she spoke as they got out of the car and walked back to where his crew was. Trina walked off and left her aunt there with them. Bay Bay was just about to run Jay down on what Trina said but a group of niggas stopped him.

"I mean damn. I know every nigga that was brought up in this hood, but none of y'all seem to come up in my memory." One of the three spoke. He was tall and dark with a long ponytail down his back and he carried the demeanor of a killer and a hustler. Jay started to let his guns do the talking but decided to keep his cool.

"Naw, we not from around here. We just came to visit our aunt, but I do like the movement y'all got going on out here," he said while giving him a hint. Jay was sitting down while everybody else was standing. He let his homies tense up and he knew that they were ready to let them have it.

"I like the movement too and I don't like when niggas come here tryna join something that don't accept new members.

Jay was pissed off now and every bit of his anger showed on his face. He stood up and pulled his strap out and his homies followed suit.

"I tried to be nice but it's always bitch niggas like you that fuck shit up. As a lil warning, me and my niggas about to set up shop and if anybody fucked up about it, we can settle this shit now," said Jay while stepping in his face.

Homeboy knew he didn't have any win, so he let Jay speak his mind.

"I'm not gonna lie when I come back shit ain't gone be sweet. Only because I'm feeling good. I'll give you a free ride up out of my shit," he said then walked off.

All Jay could do was laugh because he liked the nigga swag. They left, but before they did, they ensured them that they would be back soon.

***

Cesar, Carlos, Marisol and Pastor James were at Caesar's office. It had been years since Cesar and James sat down and talked. They were confused at what James wanted.

"What's the purpose of his meeting?" Caesar asked.

"You know exactly what I want to speak to you about."

Cesar chuckled and nodded his head. "You might as well save your breath because the kid makes me a lot of money."

"You right, this is about Peanut, and I do realize that he has his own thing going on, but he is stepping on my toes. How do you think I feel when my money being stopped because he is taking over shit that I killed for!" James yelled.

"The way I see it is he's only taking what's rightfully his. You killed your best friend in order to get where you are." Cesar shot back. James was silent as Caesar drilled him.

"You hide behind that suit and the church and still do the same shit you was doing years ago. Your time is up James, and Peanut is next in line."

"Well, you tell him if he wants war that when he gets out to be ready, 'cause what's mine don't get touched," James said as he walked out.

Marisol wasn't fazed about what was said, but it came as a surprise for Carlos. He knew nothing about what was said but now he knew James was a snake.

"Get word to Peanut about what just went down," says Caesar.

"Okay." Carlos got on his phone and walked out the office. Los would prepare Peanut, but little did he know Peanut was already ready.

Chapter 22

Peanut had become the man in county jail and was recruiting niggas left and right. With the help of his old school friend, he was getting better at being the boss he was supposed to be. Carlos had gotten word to him about Pastor James wanting to get at him. When he heard the news, it made him smile because he wondered how he got his money, cars, and clothes. He had talked to his lawyer and had gotten a year of county jail time but with a good time, he would be out in 4. He already had 2 months done. Peanut was about to give up on his drop from Carlos until he heard his name being called.

"Michael, they need you in booking." The guard called out.

"Okay," he said.

He already knew why they wanted him. He would get his weed and powder there because it was private besides a couple of inmates coming and out. He grabbed his roll of money, tucked it, then took off to booking. It took him all of 3 minutes to get there and when rounded to the corner, the same officer Carlos sent him away was waiting on him. She stood there in her tight-fitting uniform showing her every curve, and for a white girl, she was bad as hell.

"What's up sexy, you got me?" He asked as he went in the holding tank in the back. He always chose that. It was always empty and out of sitting. She processed in the few inmates and sent them on their way. By the time, she stepped in the holding tank, he was counting the roll of money.

"Half is yours and the other half is Los," he said and handed her the money.

"You don't need to pay me. Carlos does that." She handed him two packages of plastic wrap.

"If you gone pay me, pay me with this," she said while walking up to him and grabbing his dick. He had been wanting to hit that ass since the first day he saw her, so his dick instantly got hard. She wasted no time in pulling his dick out and played with it.

"Damn, yo shit is huge!"

"Don't get scared now," he said boasting. She took that as a challenge, dropped to her knees and deepthroated him all at once. Peanut stood there and took every bop like a champ and when she realized that she went into overdrive. It caught him off guard so he pulled back so he could tap the pussy. He stood her up and she quickly came out of her uniform pants. Her ass was fatter than he thought as he bent her over.

"Hurry up before somebody comes," she said looking back. He slid in with full force and speed that made here holler. She tried to run, but he locked his arms around her waist.

"Ahh! Damn. You fucking the shit out...of....me.." She moaned. "I'm coming!"

When he heard that, he sped up so he could get his too. He knew she was about to come because her pussy flexed around his dick. When it did that, they both came at the same time.

"Umm! Paid in full," she said and handed him his money back.

"Good looking out, sexy."

Hurry up and get back before it be a round two with all that good dick," she said smiling.

He fixed himself then took off back to his tank.

***

When he made it back to the tank, everybody was waiting on him. He went straight to the restroom and broke down the two packs. Then, he went to get rid of everything. As soon as he hit the rec yard, he noticed two new niggas chilling by themselves but paid them no mind. He went to his old school homie and broke him off. Everybody was coming left and right copping weed and powder from him. Peanut was so caught up in the hustle that he never noticed the two new cats moving closer and closer his way. One of Peanut's homies tapped him and put him on game just in time.

"James said back up homie," one said as walked up on him.

"Oh yeah, tell James to suck my dick, and to get your pussy ass nigga off my blocks. He got four months!" Peanut shot back. He could tell they were pissed off by what he said. He said fuck it and threw a hard left hook and knocked one smooth out. Before he could do anything else, about five goons was on both of them, stomping them out. Right then and there, he knew he had some riders on his side.

"So, what you gon' do about this nigga James?" Old School asked.

"Shoot something his way," Peanut said and walked straight to the phone.

***

Pastor James had just pulled out of the driveway and already he had a bad feeling about today. It had been exactly two weeks since he had put two niggas on Peanut to let him know to back up. He was expecting Peanut to respond back ASAP, but he didn't and that kept him on edge. The more he thought about it, the more he realized that Peanut was more like his father. He had tried to get out of the game, but it was hard because Peanut was taking over his spots and he had to do something about it.

Pastor James was so deep in his thoughts that he never noticed the blue van following him. He had been running these streets for years and he would be damned if he was gone let someone take them from him. He made up his mind that regardless of who Peanut was, he was going off him ASAP. He reached in his pocket and pulled out his phone to place a call to a person he knew would help him.

"Hey baby boy, we need to set up a meeting soon," he said.

"Cool, name the time and place so we can make it happen."

They made the arrangements then hung up the phone. He was nearing the church when he spotted Karen standing on the side of her car, and for some reason it bugged him. Right when he pulled up, he saw the blue van pass him with three young thugs in it but shrugged it off.

"What the hell you want?" He asked in frustration.

"Just came to have a little chit chat about Michael," she said. This frustrated him even more because he didn't want to talk about him. Let alone talk to her.

"What about him? He's a grown ass man."

"Okay, we don't have to talk about him, but we damn sure can talk about you," she voiced as she got out of her car and got in his face. "Let's talk about some of your old spots that you still got, which is the reason you don't talk about Michael." Karen caught him off guard with this which only pissed him off more.

Before he could say something, the blue van he saw earlier pulled up and the door slid open. When he saw the muzzle of the AR-15, he grabbed Karen and hid over behind his car as a bullet ripped through it. It seems like the gun fire took forever to stop.

"Peanut sends his regards!" He heard one of them yell before the van sped off. Karen looked at him to make sure he was okay, got in her car and left to see Peanut. James stood up dusted his suit off and at the moment, he knew shit was real.

Chapter 23

Mimi, Diamond, Jay, Bubba D, EJ, Papa, Trey, and Bay Bay sat in the living room counting up the money they had for the re-up. Everything was looking good. Mimi had doubled up the order of bricks she was getting from Carlos. While she was counting her ends, she felt eyes on her but she didn't look up because she knew exactly who it was. Carlos had already got word to her that Jay was tryna snatch the connect from up under her. She was gone tell Peanut but decided to confront him herself.

After everything was counted up, she collected the money and neatly stacked it in two small duffle bags.

"Jay, let me talk to you for a second," spoke Mimi. Everybody looked with a confused look on their face. Bubba D and her made eye contact to let him know she was good. Bubba D was loyal to her, and she liked him, which was the reason she was gone up his work out of her stash. Her and Jay stepped out back and Jay lit a cigarette.

"What's up? Talk to me."

"Me and Carlos had a talk about you not to long ago," she said.

"Look! I know you don't agree about the way Peanut got shit going, but it's his call. If you don't like it, you take it up with him."

"Look, Peanut, is getting out in a few weeks. Let's get this money and worry about this nigga James," he said and then walked back in those house."

As soon as they got in, Los and Erica walked in. Mimi and Erica instantly made eye contact and stared at each other for a lil while until Los said something.

"Mimi, how you doing? Let's get to business," he said trying to ease the tension between her and his little cousin.

"Cool, what you got for me?" She asked.

"I got forty of 'em and I understand that you got the full payment for all of them," Los said.

"Yeah, every penny. Nothing less."

He liked the way she handled her business and respected her more because she expected no handouts. She reached over, grabbed the two duffle bags and handed them to him. He looked and like what he saw. The whole crew watched as Los and Mimi handled business and was surprised at how she conducted herself as Peanut would.

Even though Jay hated to admit it, he liked what he saw and was hearing. He went out a few times then came back with the bricks two bags at a time then sat them down.

"Mami, that's a lot of work. Are you sure you can handle it?" Los asked but really was talking to everybody.

"We got a lot of spots to supply and a lot more to take over, so, of course we, can handle it," Jay spoke up, making himself known.

"Cool, just keep y'all's eyes open," he said as him and Erica made their way towards the door. Erica just couldn't make it out of the door as she looked back at Mimi.

"Make sure you tell Peanut that I love him and I'm waiting," she said and walked out.

It pissed Mimi off but she knew she was a lil girl. She made a metal note to check that ass. Jay and Trey got up then walked outside to make sure Los made it out of the hood safe. Trey had spotted an all grey Impala turning the corner slow. He warned Jay and put his hand on this .357 at the same time. They sped up but Trey never gave them a chance to start shooting as he let loose his .357. His gun was so loud that it startled Jay and made him duck for cover. The bullets put holes the size of a soda can on the car. The car kept driving at full speed.

"Damn nigga, next time warn a nigga," Jay said getting up.

"I did," Was all he said while reloading his .357. The whole crew came out with their guns drawn. Nobody got to ask nothing as the car came back around and stopped right in front of them, catching them off guard. The back window was down, and a nigga came out with a shotgun and let loose on Trey. The bullets hit Trey in his stomach knocking him off of his feet. Everybody was shocked except for Jay who started busting his twin chrome .45s, instantly killing the nigga that was hanging from the back window.

The other three doors opened and the other niggas came out blasting. They wasted no time in shooting back as they made them run back. Bubba D took off towards the car at the same time EJ did, while being cautious. One stuck his head around the car and EJ put one through his temple. Bubba D was already on the other side emptying out his clip on the other two.

James had just drawn first blood and Jay was pissed off about his homie getting killed. Jay made a promise to himself to take away everything James loved.

***

Cesar was deep in thought when Karen knocked on his office door. He had been waiting on her to come so it wasn't a surprise. It had been a long time since they last spoke, but it was still on good terms.

"Come in."

She walked in looking sexy as hell and Cesar couldn't help but stare.

"Well, hello, Cesar. Long time no see. I see you restaurants are doing good," she said.

"Yeah, and it's good to see you too. What brings you here to talk to me?" Even though he already knew, he still wanted to hear what she had to stay.

"I wanna talk to you about James."

"And." He kept it short.

"Michael's little crew almost killed me yesterday while I was tryna talk some sense into James. From the looks of it, Michael ain't letting up. At least that is what he told me yesterday. I know you have a little bit of control over James and was hoping you could talk some sense into him," she explained to Cesar.

"It's too late. What's done is done already, Mami. They both are out to kill each other. Plus, I'm on Peanut's side. This caught her off guard and all she could do was look at him.

"What do you mean?" She asked out of shock.

"James took his best friend's life out of greed and I did nothing about it. Now that this one is a man, he's taking back what is his," Cesar said calmly in his accent. She never looked at it that way and in a way, she wanted to see James die. She even went out of her way to build a solid case, but never went through with it. She was deep in thought and was snapped back when her phone rung.

"Detective Brown, "Was all she said though the phone.

"We need you in the Carson Homes. We have a homicide."

"Who?" She asked as nervousness filled her body.

"A victim by the name of Tremaine Brooks," he said. She knew him to be Michael's friend, and she knew exactly who did it.

"Okay, I'm on my way," she said and ran out of the restaurant.

Chapter 24

Jay had ducked off from the rest of the crew for the day to make a move he felt needed to be done. He really wanted to smoke the bitch Mimi, and take what was his, but he decided to go another route. He drove down I-35 with revenge on his mind. Jay thought back a year and a half ago when him and Peanut had nothing and now that they was on top, shit changed. He knew Peanut was getting out in a couple of weeks and didn't know how handle it.

If Peanut found out that he had snitched on him to save his own ass, then he would have to get ready for a shootout. He pulled up to Paradise Strip Club and the parking lot was empty except for a few cars. Jay picked this spot to meet because niggas hardly went to strip clubs during the day. He knew nobody would know. He'd sat outside for 45 minutes and contemplated on going in. He couldn't believe that he was going against the grain again, but he felt like Peanut lift him with no choice.

He finally jumped out and went inside then sat in the rear of the club. He was able to bring his strap in with the $200 he slipped the doorman. He sat his burner on his lap just in case shit went sour. One of the dancers tried to give him a dance but he waved her off. He eyed the door for at least an hour and was about to get up and leave until he spotted who he was waiting on.

"What's up baby boy? My bad for keeping you waiting so long. Just had to handle some business," he said as he sat down. Jay was pissed off and couldn't hold his tongue.

"Well, I ought to smoke yo bitch ass for getting my boy slumped," Jay as his hand tightened around his gun.

"Shit, ya boy started it and I for damn sure plan on ending it," said James as he sat down and motioned for some drinks.

The more Jay looked at James, he got pissed off at himself more and more for doing this.

"Let's get his shit over with before I change my mind and smoke yo ass in this club."

All James could do was laugh because the lil nigga was gangsta at heart but didn't have the potential to be boss. As he watched him, he could see why Peanut didn't give him the connect.

"I got a proposition for you."

"And what can a Pastor give me that I don't got?"

"I can give you yo own spots, your own crew and your own work," James stated. As soon as he finished his sentence, he knew he had him because his eyes got as big as saucers.

"And what is the catch?" Jay asked because it was always a catch.

"I want you to bring Peanut to me," he said. "Better yet I want you to kill him."

This wasn't a surprise to Jay but the surprise was that he wanted to take him up on his offer.

"And why would I do that my homie?"

James smiled because he knew Jay was dirty and grimy. "Look lil homie, just because I carry a bible and wear a suit don't mean I'm square. I been running these streets for years and I didn't get here by being innocent. I know things including the lil stunt you pulled on yo homie to get yo'self out of jail." James smirked as he told him this in street slang.

Jay started shaking because nobody was supposed to know what he'd done. He wanted to peel his shit back but decided to take him on his offer.

"If I get you what you want, keep that shit to yourself," said Jay as he tucked his heat then stood up.

"And if you don't, I'll get word to your crew on what you did. Jay walked off pissed off about what happened. He had just realized that either way it went, he had just signed his death certificate.

Chapter 25

They sat outside of the BT's off the Eastside on W.W.White. The apartment was cramped and small but they had a bunch of money coming though. Since they were so small, Bubba only brought EJ and Papa. Peanut would be coming home soon, and Bubba D wanted to make sure they owned everything. He was also recruiting niggas and putting them down with dope and spots along with the niggas Peanut was sending his way.

They all sat quiet loading up their pistol looking at everything that was going on around them. From the outside looking in, it looked easy, but neither one of them didn't care. Bubba D was snapped out of his thought when he spotted smoke gray BMW pull through the gates. When he saw who got out, he smiled and decided to wait and see what would happen.

"Say, homie ain't that fake ass Pastor?" EJ asked Bubba D from the backseat.

"Yeah, sho'll is!" He responded.

"Damn, nigga crooked than a bitch. Every spot we took over or robbed, he owns. How you think God feel about that shit?" Papa asked from the back. The question caught them off guard and they busted out laughing.

"Naw, Peanut said leave him alone until he get out, but we is gon' get everything he got."

They all hustled over to the apartment they saw him go in. Bubba D and Papa posted on one side of the door and EJ on the other side. Papa jumped off the wall to kick the door open but before he could, the door opened. Pastor James' eyes opened wide at the sight of Peanuts homies and was pissed that he got caught slipping. Papa followed through with a kick straight to his stomach knocking him on his ass.

They walked in the apartment with their guns out. To their surprise, it was only two other niggas in there. Bubba D looked around and didn't see nothing which pissed him off more.

"Tie these bitch ass niggas up," he said with anger in his voice.

"You know I own these apartments. Y'all will never leave these bitches alive," said James calmly.

Bubba D just reached over and slapped him with his strap as blood flew across the room. The shit felt so good that he slapped him again.

"Shut the fuck up before I send you to the man, foul mouth ass nigga. The only reason yo' bitch ass is still alive is because of Peanut."

James wiped the blood from his mouth and was gone say something but thought about it.

"Shake this bitch down, because I know he didn't come this way from nothing."

EJ and Papa went to the back and just like that, they found 7 bricks and a duffle bag full of hundred-dollar bills.

"Looks like we found a nice lil stash," EJ said out loud.

It was in James eyes that he was mad, but Bubba D didn't give a fuck. "Take that shit to the car so we can bounce."

EJ and Papa took the money to the car not even aware of the nigga upstairs.

"Today yo' lucky day. We just gone take yo' shit and let you keep your spot. Just know you a dead man." He told James then walked out of the door with his gun out. He jogged down a few apartments before bullets riddled the car next to him. He jumped behind it. He could hear nothing but different kinds of guns shooting his way. All he could remember was James telling him he'll never make it out alive.

The guns stopped busting but Bubba D heard footsteps coming his way. He stood up from behind the car then started shooting and dropped two niggas. He spotted one coming around the corner then let off three shots, hitting him in his chest. Niggas kept coming and he kept shooting until he ran out of bullets. He ducked back behind the car as bullets and gunfire continued to come his way. He knew his time was limited and was giving up until he saw EJ and Papa running to him with two choppas and one AR-15. They made it to him without getting hit then handed him the AR-15.

"What the fuck took you niggas so long?"

"Had to lay a couple of niggas down ourselves," said Papa.

"Let's try to get out his bitch," EJ said. They all raised up with the instinct of three natural born killers. All three of them let loose and the only guns you heard was theirs mixed with screams. They hit everything standing in their ways as they turned apartments and cars to Swiss cheese. When they ran out of bullets, the whole apartment complex as quiet and the air smelled like gun powder. When they heard the sound of police sirens, they took off to the car then peeled off.

***

Detective Karen Brown sat in the Chief of Police's office as he yelled at her.

"If you can't get this shit under control, I'll get somebody who will!" He yelled at her.

"Yes sir. I just need a little more time and I'll get to the source," she said as she stood up. She didn't want to stay there and hear his shit so she walked out and went straight her car. Michael was getting out in few days, and she wanted to keep him out of the way, but she knew he was out to get revenge. She had already made her mind up to put James's ass on the chopping block but had to before Michael put him under ground. She always knew her friend was a snake but now she was tired of his ways and wanted to put him in prison. Her phone rung and she picked it up without looking at the screen.

"Hello," she said.

"Karen, can we talk?" She knew Marisol's voice from anywhere. She couldn't stand her because she always had a crush on Gray.

"And why would you want to talk to me?" Karen asked.

"It's about James," she said.

"Well, I got to talk to someone right now. I'll call when I'm ready," Karen said then hung up the phone. She pulled out of the station then drove towards the Carson Homes. She knew it was a long shot but she had to talk to Jaylon. Things were beginning to get complicated and she was running out of options along with time.

She pulled up in front of Jay's house and his mom stepped out.

"Is Jaylon around?" She asked his mom.

"He's at his friend's house." She shot back. She already knew where that was so she jumped in her car and drove around the corner to his house. She got out then walked to the door, but before she could knock, he yelled out.

"Come in."

"She was surprised but didn't hesitate to go in.

"Jaylon, can we talk?"

"What's up?" He said while sitting down on the couch.

"I know you know who I am and what I do, but I need your help, which could help you in the long run." She explained.

"And why would I want to help the police?"

"Because I know your situation with the detectives." She went onto explain his situation about snitching. He laughed excuse everybody seem to know about this situation and wanted to help, but in the wrong way. He got pissed off and grabbed his .45 off the table and pointed it at her forehead.

"How about I blow ya head off for tryna play me, bitch!" He said with anger in his eyes.

"You could do that and do a life sentence, or you could help you and your best friend out by bringing down James." He hesitated before he put the gun away. "Talk to me and be straight up with me."

Chapter 26

A couple weeks had passed, and Peanut was walking out of the county jail in the same thing he got locked up in which now smelled dingy and stale. He stretched and took in the fresh air then took off walking towards downtown. He didn't let no one know he was getting out so he could have time to think.

Peanut had noticed a white Mercedes on 26 inch rims circle around a couple of times. When the Mercedes finally stopped on the side of him, he got nervous. He saw the passenger side door open, and Mimi came running around to him full speed. She jumped on him full force, wrapped her legs around his waist and kissed him deeply. He put her down then looked at her and saw that she was sexier than the last time he saw her. She had on a Pink St. Laurent thigh high dress, some pink and white heels and Peanut wondered how she ran in them.

"I missed you baby," she said looking down.

"I missed you too, and why you looking shy?"

"Nothing just happy to see you, but you smell like jail. Let's get you home so you can change," she said.

"Who ride is that?"

As soon as he asked, Diamond rolled down the window.

"Damn, lil mama, you balling like that?" He asked smiling.

"Shit, you know how we do. Just wait until you see yours," Diamond said.

He got in and Mimi was right next to him.

"I know you need some of that," Diamond said as she pulled off then passed him a Sweet. He hit it like he never hit a Sweet before and damn near coughed his lungs up. All they could do was laugh as he hit it again.

"Catch me up on what's going on," He spoke.

"All you need to know is that you the boss of some loyal niggas except for one. We got a new crib, new whips and everything."

"Cool," he said while shaking his head.

"Once you handle yo business at home, you can meet ya squad," voiced Mimi. They pulled up to a two-story house with a black-on-black BMW on some 26 inch Forgiotto rims. He jumped out then looked in the inside and saw what it was decked out.

"Let's see how the bedroom look." He whispered in Mimi's ear. By the time they made it upstairs to the bedroom, Mimi was already naked. She was so fine that he just stopped and stared at her.

"Are you gone come handle up? You scared?" He took his shirt off and she gasped because he was stacked with muscles and marked with tattoos.

"Not so skinny no more."

"Damn!" was all she could say as she kissed down his body while undoing his pants. He was finally naked when she saw his dick for the first time ever.

"Damn, I can't believe I been missing out on this big ol' muthafucka!" She played with it and then made love to his dickhead with her tongue. She bopped up and on his dick deep throating him liked a champ. She felt him about to come and sped up as he shot everything down her throat. He lied her on the bed and put her legs over his shoulder.

He sucked on her clit as she squirmed and moaned in ecstasy.

"This shit taste as good as it looks." He went overtime licking, sucking, and finger fucking her pussy as she busted all over his tongue. He hovered over her pussy as he entered his dick slowly in here.

"It's been a long time daddy so be easy," she said as she braced herself for all eight and a half inches. As he worked himself inside, her moans became louder because it was too much.

"Oh! Daddy! Oh baby, fuck me!" She moaned out loud. He sped up and pounded harder as her pussy gripped his dick. Her pussy was so wet that juices flowed down his dick to his nuts.

"This daddy pussy, ain't it? Damn, this pussy tight as fuck!" He flipped her over plunged back in and smacked her ass as it jiggled.

"Yeah, baby this you pussy and only ours. Oh! Ahh! Ahh! I can't take no more baby. It's too much!" She screamed as she came on his dick. Before he could get good into fucking her from behind, she moved and got on top. She got flat on her feet as she bounced up and down on just the head. She decided to stop playing games and made sure he never wanted to leave. She rode his dick like a pro. He just laid there in pleasure as they both came with each other.

***

Peanut had fell asleep then woke up at 12:00 am and decided to check in with the homies. Nobody knew he was home and he wanted to keep it like that. He drove by all of his spots just to peep out the scene and was satisfied. Mimi had done a good job while he was gone, especially getting a crib that nobody knew about. He had pulled up to his hood and was happy to be back in action. He knew everybody would be here because Mimi called and told them to come. He parked then reached under the seat and grabbed his .40 Cal then tucked it. The first person he spotted was Jay's snake ass and it hurt his feelings.

Everybody eyed the car because nobody knew who it was. Bubba D was the first to pull out his heat and that's when he stepped out. When Jay saw Peanut step out, his eyes got big as saucers as he thought he was seeing things. Everybody was happy to see Peanut as they greeted him. They all give him daps and hugs, but he only was focused on Jay.

"What's up homie?" Jay said.

"What's good my nigga?" He said keeping his cool. He chatted with the crew as they caught him up on things.

"Let me holla at you for second, Jay."

Jay said nothing as he followed him to the car and then got in.

"Talk to me, baby." Peanut lit up a Newport to calm his nerve. "So, what's up with this nigga James?" He asked.

Shit, the homies just got at the nigga the other day but left him alive for you," said Jay.

"That's what's up. What about the spots and the new niggas."

"Same ol, same ol. Look, I'm glad you home my nigga. Shit didn't feel right when you was absent."

"I know but now that I'm back, shit about to get real. If niggas is foul or was fucked up about how things was, I'll deal with it fa'sho. All need to know is you ready for war."

"Hell yeah!" He said as he pulled out his strap. "I stay ready!"

"Already, I got to meet up with Los to let him know I'm back in charge," he said hoping he caught every bullet he shot his way.

Jay got out of the car and Peanut was happy to get him out of his presence. He cut the music down then headed to Los's spot. As he drove in silence, he plotted a million different ways to get at Jay and James. With James, he needed a gang of niggas, but since he knew Jay and James had hooked up, he would find a way for Jay to bring them together.

Chapter 27

Los had talked to Peanut a couple of days ago to set up a meeting and put him up on game. He had missed Peanut being around and couldn't wait to chop it up. It was 8:00 pm and Los had just pulled in Paradise Strip Club. It was busy as usual which made Los grab his Glock 9 and stuck it in his pants. He got out then stood on the side of his truck and smoked a cigarette. Then, he walked through the door. Before he walked in, he saw Peanut pull up and park. Los walked to the back table so he could watch every angle of the club.

For some reason, he didn't feel right and wanted to leave, but thought twice when a bad bitch rolled up on him.

"Hey daddy, you need some company?" She asked.

"Not really, but if you have a homegirl, me and my homie don't mind y'all being around," Los said.

"Just chill, I'll be right back," she said then quickly walked off. As soon she left, Peanut came then walked straight to where he was.

"What's up, Papi? You looking good, how you been?" Los said as he stood up and showed him some love.

"I'm good now that I'm home and ready to get back on track," Peanut stated.

The stripper that left came back with a girl that was ten times badder that she was.

"Let's have some fun first then we can talk and catch up," Los said as the two girls came their way.

"Fa'sho." Was all Peanut could say.

When City Girls and Cardi B song came on, both strippers got on stage and shook their asses as they threw 20s on them. While they danced, Peanut couldn't help but talk about business.

"So, what's up with James?" He asked.

"All I know is that he's preparing for you. Don't know how but be ready. As far as money, Mimi has been doing good," He said as he kept dropping money.

Peanut shook his head in an agreement because he had a team of niggas ready to ride for the cause. The song was over and one of the girls got off stage and grabbed Peanut. Then, took him to the back. He sat down and watched as lil mama twerked her ass in his face. He pulled his gun out and sat it behind him so she couldn't see it. She turned around then straddled his lap and went to work while he pulled her titties out and stuffed his face in them.

The music was loud, but Peanut still heard the click from the door open. He made no sudden movement as he slowly reached behind him for his heat. Peanut saw the big nigga come in slow and noticed he was the nigga from the door. As soon as the nigga got close, Peanut slung ol' girl to the floor and shot him twice in the head. Ol' girl screamed when she saw blood leaking out the back of his head.

"You stupid bitch!" He said as he slapped her then put one in her head. "Next time set the right one up!" As he stepped over the big nigga and walked out, he heard multiple gun shots up front. He ran with his gun out because he knew Los was in trouble. He spotted Los ducking behind one of the stages as one nigga was steady busting his way. Peanut ran up behind him and put one if the back of his head. Everybody was running out of the way of the bullets which made it easier to spot the rest of the shooters.

Los came from behind the stage shooting at the back exit as niggas came though. He dropped them one by one as

Peanut covered the front of the club. Los reloaded and Peanut conserved his bullets because he was limited.

"Los we got to go, let's make our way out." He yelled over the gunshots.

Los said nothing and started towards the door. When they made it to the door, they thought they were in the clear until bullets came flying their way. They both hid on the side of the building.

"What the fuck is that?" Los asked.

"Gotta to be James," he whispered. Peanut peeped around the corner and three niggas had on masks and one of them caught this eye. For some reason, the nigga moved familiar, but he paid it no attention and started shooting their way. They both shot their guns until it was empty. The niggas didn't let up off their triggas as Peanut and Los made it to their whips and peeled. Peanut followed Los to one of his spots on the west side and finally felt ease. James had sunt people his way and now it was his turn.

***

Big Mama, Mrs. James and Hazel was on their way to meet Peanut for the first time since he'd been home. Big Mama was happy to see him, but Hazel was happier. It had been a long time since she'd seen him and she missed him. She had liked him and intended on letting him know today. She had on a blue jean Polo skirt and a khaki and brown Polo blouse that brought her Hazel eyes out more. He khaki Louis Vuitton high heels matched her Louis Vuitton purse, and her hair was pressed back in a ponytail. They pulled up in Applebee's and didn't realize that they parked right next to Peanut. They got out and started walking towards the door. Peanut rolled down his window and couldn't help but call Hazel's name. She was petite and sexy and when she turned around they locked eyes and she smiled.

"Boy get yo butt out of that car and where you get that high dollar car from anyway?" Big Mama asked him.

He stepped out in some smoke gray cargo capri pants, a black and white Polo striped shirt. His white Air Force Ones showed off his black Nike socks. His tripled matching gold earrings, watch, and chain glared off the sun as he walked towards them. He hugged Big Mama first, Mrs. James then Hazel. She seemed to hug him tight as they both smelled each other.

"How you doing Hazel?" He asked her.

"I'm alright, how about yourself?" She asked. For some reason, he wanted to tell her everything but knew he couldn't.

"Everything all good now. Let's go eat I'm starving." They walked in Applebee's and sat at the table next to the side window. He sat next to Hazel as Big Mama and Mrs. James sat across from them. They caught up and laughed at each other and Peanut felt comfortable at the moment. An hour had past and Big Mama and Mrs. James said they had to be at church. Hazel grabbed Peanut's hand and squeezed it. She didn't know when she was gone see him again and wanted to kick it with him some more.

Peanut caught the gesture and spoke up.

"Well, can Hazel kick it with me for a while? I'll make sure I have her home early."

Mrs. James looked at them both then Big Mama and finally decided to say yes.

"You keep her safe," Mrs. James said as they got up to leave.

Peanut and Hazel followed, and they got in his BMW.

"Peanut this car is nice. Where did you get if from?" She asked.

"It was a welcome home gift. So, what you want to do? Everything is on me?"

"It don't matter I just want to be around you," she said shyly.

"Girl, this is not what you want."

"How you know what I want when you never asked?"

"Because I know my lifestyle ain't fit for yours," he said.

"It's not, but it never stopped me from liking you."

He said nothing as she leaned over to kiss him. Her lips felt soft, so he fell right into it. They kissed for a whole minute before he pulled away from her.

"Damn girl, don't get nothing started."

"And if I do?" She smiled."

Alright girl, keep on. Come on its 12:00 pm. The Spurs come on at 2:00 pm. Let's get some snacks and go chill."

"You got some weed?" He looked at her, smiled and nodded his head as he pulled off.

Chapter 28

Los was sitting in his uncle's house with 10 other goons he had called together. The little stunt that James had pulled at the strip club had cost James a lot.

"Sabrino, are you sure you want to do this?" Ceasar asked.

Los said nothing as she sat there and loaded up his AK47.

Caesar picked up his phone to make sure Peanut was ready.

"Talk to me," said Peanut.

"My nephew is certain that James is behind all this and wants to pay him a visit."

"As do I."

"Well, I don't want him just yet. I want something that will hurt him."

"What do yo have in mind?" He asked.

"Where he stays, there's a shed with a basement hidden underneath with his money, weed, and powder. Basically, his life savings. You go get that and Los will kill off his main spot." Cesar explained.

"Sounds good. Tell Los to let me know what's good on his side."

"Okay," he said and hung up.

Los and his crew loaded up in two separate vans with 5 apiece. Then, they drove to the Northeast side of town. Los sat in the back in all black with is AK47 in his lap. It had been years since Los had to get back in his murderous ways. In Puerto Rico, Los was part of a goon squad that killed tons of people. Now that he was in San Antonio and was a drug lord, he put to rest his old ways.

The ride to the Northeast said was quiet and fast due to him driving 90 miles per hour in a 70 miles per hour speed limit. They pulled up to some house that was ducked off into the back of some apartments that looked abandoned. From the way they drove in, the house looked dead too, until they made their way to the middle. They parked then sat to watch the movement for a little while to make sure they covered each other.

The block they was on was like a movie and looked like it was a party going on. It was bitches everywhere and slabs parked up and down the block. Music was bumping loud as bitches shook their asses on niggas.

Los peeped every angle to see if he saw James but didn't. He knew he wouldn't be here but hoped to have a chance to dead the nigga himself.

"Alright, let's make sure every nigga out here is dead!" Said Los to his team of killers. They all moved down the block with AK's and AR's Nobody seemed to notice them until Los let loose on the house that had a few niggas on the porch. The AK47 ripped holes in every nigga that was there and chopped the house up like it was the enemy. Niggas came running their way shooting hand guns, but they street sweepers made sure that they didn't make it too far. Hoes and niggas took off running each and everyway they could to get out of the way of death. Los was in a zone and was snapped out of it when brains hit him in his face.

He realized that it was one of his men and got even more mad. He looked around and spotted movement on the side of a parked car. He move so fast that the nigga never saw him come around the other end.

"Too bad you bitch ass is on the wrong side," said Los as he pressed the trigga on his AK and held it down so six bullets tore open his chest. He kept it moving, shooting his AK until it was empty. Los dropped it, pulled out a set of

9mms and started firing at anybody who wasn't with him. Niggas along with women hit the ground with holes in their bodies.

The scene was quiet expect for the music coming from cars. They still held their guns just in case niggas was still hiding. Even though one of them died, they still felt like something wasn't good.

***

Peanut, Bubba D, and Jay had just stepped out of the dope fiend rental and hustled down the street.

Peanut brought a couple of duffle bags just in case they needed them. He looked at Jay and that's when he was gone get to James without him knowing. He wanted to off the nigga soon as possible.

When they got to the house, all the lights were off. "We got to be quite as possible so we don't wake nobody up," Said Peanut.

They made it toward the back and it didn't take them long to get inside of the basement. The lil basement was full of money, weed, and powder. Most of the weed and money was bagged up so they dumped the bricks in the duffle bags they had. They even took the few guns that was on the far wall. It took them a few trips to take everything back to the car. Peanut stayed back just in case James stumbled on him. Everything was done and they made their way back to the car.

"Jay, I got a plan," Said Peanut. He looked nervous and Peanut saw it. Now, he finally realized Jay was the nigga James sent to Paradise to kill him. Now that he knew that he knew his plan would work perfect. He said nothing else as he dialed Los's number.

"Yeah, we on our way back."

'Okay, we just finished up here."

"You think he'll come to us?" Peanut asked.

"I don't know."

"If he don't, I know how to get him to," he said then hung up and plotted some more on James and Jay.

Chapter 29

Detective Brown wasn't sure if it was the house and drove around before she realized it was it. Mimi had given her the info to get to the house so she could talk to Peanut. She knew it was a long shot, but she had to at least talk to Peanut again. She pulled up to the beautiful house with three beautiful cars in front. She knew he was doing good but didn't know it was this good. Karen got out and the door opened before she even got there.

Mimi was standing in the doorway looking beautiful even in her pajamas.

"I'm sorry, I know its early but I need to talk to him."

"Come in." She walked in and Peanut came from down stairs in just his basketball shorts. She stopped and stared at him because he was handsome and fine a hell. He looked just like Gray, which made her have a sudden urge for him.

"What's up? What you doing here? How did you know where I stayed?" He asked questions back and back. Mimi had already let her know Peanut didn't want nobody to know where they stayed so she was quick on her feet.

"Michael, I'm a detective. I came to talk to you and see how you was doing."

He looked from her to Mimi and knew something was up.

He sat down on the couch and turned on the news. She sat next to him and watched as well.

"So, what you want to talk about?" He asked then lit a Newport. He felt weird sitting in his living room with a law, but knew it couldn't been no different from sitting with Jay.

"About you."

"And what might that be about?"

"You got a lot of shit going on in the streets and the Chief of Police don't like that. They want me to bring you down, but you know I don't want to do that. Now, I do want to bring down James and I want to do it before you do anything crazy." She explained.

He laughed because his mind was already made up and what he was gon' do.

"We both know that this nigga and his snitch ass protege gots to die. It can't be an alternative."

"I talked to Jay. He's willing to bring James to me so you could go free," she said.

"Not too surprising on his behalf. Now what's crazy is I'm gon' use him for the same thing. No matter what happens, to me they both gotta go."

Before she could say something, she heard breaking news on the T.V.

"Breaking News just came in from the Northeast Side of town. It seems to be bodies all over the place along with 10 times as many shell casings. The police was called this morning in what seems to be a street massacre. Everything on the streets has bullet holes or blood on it. Nothing was taken as police collected tons of money and drugs." The reported continued to explain.

She looked from the T.V. to Peanut and Peanut did the same. As soon as he heard the reporter, he already know who it was that was behind the massacre.

"I know you know who was behind it, but I'm not gon' even ask," she said. At that moment, her phone rung. She didn't want to pick it up because she knew it was the Chief of Police.

"Yes sir," Was all she said to answer the phone.

"Get to the crime scene and handle the situation!" He yelled.

"Yes sir," she said then hung up. "Look just stay out of the way until I figure something out." She raced out of the door, jumped in her car then sped off. She was so in a hurry that she didn't see the car get behind her. She got on Hwy 290 and hit her lights so he could get there quick as possible. She got to the crime scene in no time and what she saw made her stop. There were dead bodies everywhere. Some had lots of bullet holes and some just had one shot to the head. She had to tip toe or walked slowly around the scene so she wouldn't get blood on her shoe or step on shell casings. They collected bullets and blood samples but didn't have no witnesses to question.

She knew who this block belonged to because he purchased the house when she was on his payroll. She knew now that it was to a point of no return. She just hoped that Michael came through it all.

***

When he followed Karen back to his main spot and saw that this block was surrounded with bodies and cops, it boiled his blood. After the incident that happened in the BT's, he was staying low. Something told him to follow Karen and he came up with where Peanut stayed. He knew exactly who was behind this. He had fucked up when he sent his boys to get at Peanut while Los was with him. It was time to call a meeting with his crew to let them know that everything was a go. Before he could make the call, his phone rung and an unrestricted number popped up.

"Hello," he said through the phone.

"Consider what you got a little warning about what I'ma do to your hating ass," said Peanut.

"Ha! Boy you just signed your death certificate."

"My pops died by your hand so I'ma make sure I repay the favor. And I knew about yo lil flunky, Jay too. Y'all make a good couple since both of y'all hate on y'all best friends."

"I own these streets, lil nigga. You want what's mine? Come take it!" He yelled.

"Oh, I already did that, homie. Just watch yo back cause I'ma coming sooner that you think." Peanut laughed and hung up.

He didn't even look tampered with, but he knew better. He opened it up and went in the basement.

"AAAHHH!" He yelled. He yelled so loud that Mrs. James came running out.

When she realized what he was yelling about, she was mad because he lied to her. Peanut had overstepped his boundaries this time. He had a plan and was gone do this one by himself. He picked up his phone and dialed Cesar's number.

"You sent your people to my block!" He said with pure anger.

"You sent your people to kill my nephew," Cesar a shot back.

"I didn't know he was going with him. Just stay out of my way this time."

"It's too late. You almost killed what was mine. Now, your my enemy too," he said with a strong accent then hung up the phone.

He called up his team for a meeting then called Peanut back but got no answer. James was so angry that he didn't even hear Mrs. James talking to him. His past came roaring back as he yelled curse words one after another. He took off to his car and peeled off towards the East Side. On his way, he grabbed his 9mm out of the glove compartment and sat it on his lap. Not sure about what he was gone do when he got there, but something had to be done. His phone had rung, and he saw that it was Karen.

"I'm guessing you calling me about my block." He asked.

"Yep, seeing that at first you were out of the game and I'm guessing you know who did it."

"I do but none of that shit matters cause when I see him, I'ma bury the lil nigga next to his daddy!"

"You stupid muthafucka. You watch your mouth. He was your best friend, and he's just a kid!" She yelled though the phone.

"Not no more."

"Well if that's the case, you better watch your back cause if he don't kill you, I'ma lock yo snake ass up for life!" She yelled and hung up. He was pissed and pulled over on the side of the freeway. His past was catching up to him and it only had one ending.

Chapter 30

Jay was sitting on the stoop making sale after sale as he smoked a Sweet to himself. He was the only one there so his pockets was looking good. He hadn't heard from James since he tried to murk Peanut and lost that night at Paradise. From his understanding, Peanut didn't expect nothing since he gave everything they hit James for to him and the crew. He spotted a tall white girl coming his way and couldn't help but stare. As she move closer and closer, he saw how fine she was and stood up.

"What's up sexy? You look out of place over this way. Who you with?" Jay asked while licking his lips.

"I'm by myself. I just moved down the street and just wanted to check out the neighborhood," she said.

"Well, my name is Jay and if you need anything let me know."

"My name is Sarah and I do need something."

"And what might that be?"

"I need some weed and I can smell that down the street," she said. He smiled because he knew that was his chance to try and fuck.

"Okay, well come in and we can smoke as much as you want."

She walked in and before she walked in, she looked down the street and gave a quick head nod. When she walked in, she sat next to him then grabbed the blunt he was already smoking. She barely hit it and coughed then passed it back.

He got closer and started rubbing on her legs. She didn't like it but she played along as she kept looking out of the door. He buried his face into her neck and was so caught up in her, that he never noticed Peanut and EJ slide in.

Peanut tiptoed to the back of Jay, eased the Mossberg pump up then came down hard on the back of his head knocking him out. They lifted Jay off of ol' girl then tied him up.

"How much I owe you sexy?" He asked while pulling out a roll of money.

"How many times I gotta tell you I don't want yo money. Just give me some dick and we good," she said.

He cut for lil momma since he met her in county jail and was gone break her off anyway. Him and EJ grabbed Jay then carried him to the car and stuffed him in their truck. Peanut had told everybody to fall back and meet him in Spring Hill Apartments. They had a spot where they would take Jay and expose him.

All of them jumped in the car then smashed off towards Spring Hill. He grabbed up his phone and dialed Bubba D. He must have been waiting on his call because he answered ASAP.

"What's up? Talk to me," Said Bubba D.

"Yeah, we on our way. Just make sure everybody there," said Peanut then hung up. He didn't plan on killing him just yet, but planned on him getting James to come his way. They drove in silence and thought about what he was gone do to James once he caught him. He was gone let Jay sit and think about being a snake ass nigga for a couple of days. His phone rung and he answered it quick.

"Los, what's up baby?"

"You tell me. I got a real big package for you," he said.

"Where you want to meet?" Peanut asked.

"At baby girl's house." When he said that, he knew he was talking about Erica. It had been months since he seen or heard from her.

"Okay, gimme like an hour and I'll be there."

"Cool, Papi," he said then hung up.

He pulled in the last entrance and drove straight to the back. By it being close to dark, a few people was out, but they had nothing to worry about. Him and EJ got out then pulled Jay out of the trunk and carried him inside. Everybody was there including Mimi and Diamond. They sat him in a chair then tied him to it. Papa came with a bucket of water and splashed it on his face. The water woke him up immediately and his eyes adjusted to everybody in his crew standing around him. He knew exactly where he was because it was his idea to set the spot up.

"What the fuck is wrong with niggas and how the fuck did I get here?"

It was no need to answer his questions as he noticed the white girl and Peanut standing next to each other.

"Nigga don't act like you don't know what the fuck this is!" said Peanut. "Nigga you was my best friend and you told on me."

"It wasn't even like that," he said with his head down.

Peanut reached back and punched the nigga in the face knocking him over. He started kicking him in the stomach over and over. "You! Stupid! Mutherfucka! Who! Do! You! Think! I! Am!" He yelled while kicking him viciously. Jay was coughing up blood by the time Peanut stopped kicking him. Two of Peanut lil homies picked up the chair.

"I would ask you why you did it that don't matter. The question is, why you switch sides?" Asked Peanut.

"Fuck that nigga. I didn't do shit for the nigga."

Peanut laughed because the nigga he knew to be his best friend was now dead to him. Peanut pulled his 40 Cal out and touched Jay's forehead with the tip.

"Yo bitch ass tried to smoke me and Los outside of Paradise. I know how you move, so don't lie," he said. "I really want to put a bullet in yo shit so bad, but I need you to call James and tell him you got me." He pulled Jay's cell phone from his pocket, dialed James' number and handed it to him.

"You know what to say," said Peanut with is 40 Cal to his head. It rung a couple to times before James answered.

"What's up lil nigga?"

"Yo, guess who I got for you?" said Jay.

"Who might that be?"

"I got Peanut, but I need a few day so I can get him where I need him."

"Cool, call me back in a couple of days with where you gone have him," said James.

"Alright, I'll holla at you."

Peanut pulled the phone away, hung it up, then put it back in his pocket.

"Leave this nigga here, then bring him to me so we can end this shit," he said before he walked off.

***

James sat across the street with one of his homies from back when him and Gray first started this shit. They watched as Los walked to the house without a care in the world. He checked Kay that was sitting in his lap for the fifth time before his homie said something.

"So, what you gone do?"

"I just wanna send Cesar a warning," he said. "That ain't shit sweet." He stepped out with Kay and stood in the middle of the street. He waited a lil bit before he squeezed the trigga. The shot was so loud that he never heard the car park down the street. He held the trigga down until every bullet was gone. James felt a quick adrenaline rush as he stood there. He was snapped back to reality when he heard the car door slam.

When he saw Peanut running his way, he panicked and ran to his car.

Peanut busted his 40 Cal and shattered the back window. Bullet holes decorated the back to the car as he peeled off. He wanted to chase James, but he need to check on Los. Before he got there, Erica and Marisol came running out.

"Where's Los?" was all he asked.

"He's shot, Papi. Somebody shot him," said Erica.

"Is he dead?"

"No!" Marisol said crying.

Peanut was mad that Los got shot so he took off with the intention on speeding up the process of killing James.

Chapter 31

Peanut pulled up to the house to pick up Hazel but had his strap on his lap in case James came out. He had made his mind up that whenever he saw James, he was dead on sight. He blew the horn and two minutes later, Hazel came out in some blue Jean shorts, a purple Alexandre McQueen top, some purple low top Converses. He hair was tied back in a ponytail which showed her hazel eyes. He was so mesmerized that he didn't notice her open the door.

"Hey Michael, you okay?" she asked.

"Yeah, just admiring how beautiful you are."

"He didn't realize how thick she was until she walked out in those shorts.

She got in and kissed him. When she kissed him, her pussy got wet just by his lips touching hers.

"What do you got planned since you on paying?" He asked as she drove off.

She pulled out a blunt and looked at him then lit it.

"I didn't know you smoked like that."

"I been smoking for years; I just keep it from my dad," she said, while pulling out a bag of Doe-doe. "I'm really tryna kick it at your spot again. I just want to chill, smoke, and watch you make money."

"Girl, you know anything can happen in the Carson Homes."

"I know but I just wanna see what you do and be around you. I've been liking you for a long time and now I got my chance to show you." She explained.

"You know yo daddy don't cut for me too much so if he find out about us, it's over."

"It don't matter because he does the same thing you do."

He looked at her in shock because he didn't know she knew. She explained to him on what had happened to her dad, which Peanut know already because he did it. They talked which made their ride seem shorter. Peanut didn't know if anyone was there, so he told her to wait outside. Nobody was there as he checked inside and told her to come in. She sat down on the couch as Peanut got situated. She was startled when somebody knocked on the door. Peanut came rushing out to the back with his pistol and answered the door. He relaxed when he saw it was one of his clientele."

"Damn baby boy, you gone shoot me?" He asked nervously.

"Naw, I just got to be on point these days. What you need?"

"Let me get $100 worth, and if I can, that beautiful woman."

"That's off limits right, but I got you on the first offer."

Hazel smiled at them both while she watched him do business. She was already turned on by him coming out with his gun, and now that she saw him conduct business, she was horny all over. When he came and sat down next to her, she wanted no time and straddled him.

"Girl, don't start no shit," he said as he wrapped his arms around her lower back.

"Michael, I want you to take my virginity," she said while looking him in the eyes.

He said nothing back as he kissed her passionately.

She raised his shirt over his head and started kissing his chest. "Mmm! You're so sexy," she said.

He raised up and put her on the couch then slowly undressed her. He had her down to her bra and panties and saw that she was nervous.

"Don't worry, baby girl. I got you." He took off her bra and panties then sucked on her beautiful titties.

"Oh!" She moaned.

He kissed his way down her stomach as he made his way to her shaved pussy. He went to work as he smelled the juices coming from her pussy. He knew she hadn't felt anything like this so he took his time.

"Oh! My! God! Ahh! Michael, it feels good!" She screamed. "I'm...I'm...." She squirmed and tried to get away as she came in Michael's mouth. He lapped up every drop that came out of her pussy. He stood up and dropped his pants and boxers all at once. When she saw the size of his dick, she gasped.

"Damn, Michael!" She said as her eyes got big.

"I got you. Just trust me." He raised her knees to her chest and looked her in the eyes. He guided his dick in her slowly as she tried to get away.

"Ahh! Oh shit." She screamed in pleasure.

He only had half of his dick in her when she saw white cream on his dick. He knew she was coming because she was shaking. He didn't stop and put his whole dick in her with one stroke.

"Oh, baby. Fuck me baby! Let me feel you!"

He sped up a little bit but had to pace himself because her pussy was so tight. He stood up then laid her over the arm of the couch and her juicy pussy popped out at him. Her ass was fat, and he entered her then long stroked her. She damn near climbed over the couch as he pounded her pussy.

"I'm coming again, daddy! It feels so good baby. Yes! Yes!" She yelled. He smacked her ass as he sped up.

"Come in me!" She threw her ass back at him, and when she did that, she felt him in her stomach. It felt like she felt him grow more as he filled her pussy full of come. They laid on the couch naked as she kissed him. He laid there with thoughts of killing her daddy and she didn't even know it.

***

James and five of his goons were parked down the street loading up guns. He didn't know how this situation would turn out to be, but he had to try. James knew that if he killed Cesar that it would make focusing on Peanut a lot easier. They jumped out of the van with no ski masks and made their way down the street. He had shot Los but didn't kill him, so he had to get at Cesar before he got at him.

They spotted two guards standing in front of the gates. The guards noticed movement then drew their guns and immediately started shooting. James in front, let his UZI go, killing both guards. He knew that Cesar didn't have that many guards so once they got in, it would be easy. They had to jump the gate to get in and were surprised by the gunshots coming from up above. James dove behind some bushes as he saw two of his guys gunned down. The other three who killed the shooters on the balcony. Now four deep, they made their way to the house shooting anything in their path.

When they got in the house, it was quiet which made him nervous. He spotted somebody behind a corner and shot his way. The person shot back their way, hitting one of the goons in his head, killing him instantly. James ran full speed up the stairs and killed the shooter. He opened every door looking for Cesar, even though he knew where he was.

He had finally made it to his office and spotted Cesar smoking a cigar.

"You know that you won't live through this situation, right?" He asked James.

"I don't care but when you messed with my money you had to know you wouldn't survive either," Said James as he pointed his gun towards Cesar. Cesar stood up and started shooting their way. James dove outside of the office while the other two got gunned down. When Cesar was out of bullets, James came back in, but Cesar was ducked behind the desk. James walked around the desk and saw that he was shot in the arm. Memories came flooding black as he stood over Cesar.

"Tell Gray I said what's up," he said as he emptied his clip into Cesar's body. He hustled out of the house one deep then made his way back to where he was parked.

Chapter 32

The word about Ceasar getting killed had gotten to Peanut quick. Even though it had been a couple of days, he was finally getting after James. He sat in one of Los's trap houses on the Westside along with at least fifty other niggas. Niggas was fucked up about Ceasar being killed and wanted to do something about it. Los sat in the far corner smoking a blunt. He was pissed off about not being able to go after James himself, due to him being shot in the stomach.

He was now the head nigga in charge and would hold it down. He already knew he would make Peanut his right-hand man.

"Alright, everybody let's get down to business!" Peanut yelled out to everybody. It took a couple of minutes for everybody to get inside because there were so many of them. Some lit up blunts and some poured up Cîroc to numb their feelings. Peanut gave Los a head nod so he could start.

"By now, everybody in San Antonio knows about my uncle being killed. Some niggas might try us and some niggas might move on and do their own thing. But I promise it won't be easy. Now, the nigga James got to die," Los said as he gave the floor to Peanut.

"Nobody needs to worry about James because here in the next couple of hours, his ass is good as smoked. I got one of his lil homies, which use to be one of us. He is good as dead next to James. Now, I got the part under control, but we must be ready for a war because the nigga James ain't just anybody." Explained Peanut.

"Man fuck that nigga. When you find him, let me smoke his bitch ass!" One of them yelled out.

"That's the attitude I need, but James is mine but y'all can do whatever y'all want to Jay's snitch ass."

They was in full conversation when someone knocked on the door. Los and Peanut both looked at each other with a confused look.

"You expecting somebody?" Peanut asked Los.

"Naw," he said as he pulled out his banger then looked out of the peephole. He looked back at Peanut with a surprised look on his face before he opened up the door for Marisol and Detective Brown.

"What the fuck type of shit is this?" Peanut asked Marisol.

'It ain't even like that. Just hear her out and I promise y'all won't be mad." Marisol told them both. Before they could say anything, Karen spoke up.

"I know y'all feel like y'all know the streets, but I know them better. I used to be a strong part of your daddy's operation along with Marisol here, but that's another story," said Karen.

"James did some snake shit back then and still doing it now. I see that your best friend is doing it now and she wants to help, but like she did for Gray and James," said Marisol.

Peanut was still looking at them crazy until it dawned on him that she used to be on his pop's payroll. He look at Los and nodded his head in an approving way. Peanut was always quick at picking up this, which was why he was where he was at so quick. Los trusted Peanut and gave him the go ahead.

"That sounds nice and trust me, we gon talk but right now we need to handle this situation before it gets out of hand," said Peanut.

"Cool, just handle your end and I'll make sure my end stays out of the way," she said, giving him the green light. He turned around then got back to business as they walked out. He had a million thoughts running through his head. The game was moving fast but he knew it would be like this, and that's what he was taught by old school in jail. They finished up the meeting and the Peanut pulled Los to the backyard so they could talk.

"What was that all about, Papi?" Los asked Peanut.

"You know Detective Brown used to work for my dad and wants to work for us. Los, after all this is done, I'll explain everything. Just trust me."

"I can do. Just get this nigga James," Los said while giving him dap then walked back inside. Peanut knew that with the police on his side they could be unstoppable. He began to put a plan together and knew he would elevate.

***

Papa had just got a call from Peanut that he's pulling up. It was 7:30 am and Peanut had plans on James meeting Jay at the church. He knew James would be comfortable in a church but little did he know all hell would break loose. Jay came walking towards the car in the same clothes he had on for the past three days.

"What's up homie!" Said Jay as he got in the rental car. Peanut pulled out his pistol and sat it his lap.

"Bitch ass nigga, I ain't ya homeboy. Snitches and disloyal niggas don't got no place in my heart. The only reason you still alive is so I can get to that punk ass patna of yours," he said. "I need you to call and tell him to meet you at his church." He handed him his phone back then waited till he called James. He explained to James why he wants to meet him at the church and he won't do it.

He just doesn't know that his life would end up aligned with James' life. He tightened his hand around his gun then pulled off towards the church.

Chapter 33

James had just pulled up to the church not knowing about the set up. The church was empty every morning at his tune and that's why he agreed to meeting here. He tucked one gun behind his back and kept one in his hand as he entered the church. He pulled out his phone to look at the text Jay had just sent him, which said that he was just down the street. James went to sit on the front pew then placed a call to one of his goons.

"Is everybody in place?" He asked through the phone.

"Yeah, we're ready just in case some shit pop off." He felt satisfied and hung up. As soon as he put his phone in his pocket, Jay came walking through the door. With his hand on his gun, he swept the room quickly with his eyes. He was nervous as he walked to James then sat next to him.

"So, how did we get Peanut?" He asked Jay.

"He's supposed to be meeting me in a few minutes. I just wanted to make sure I was ready."

"Lil nigga don't fuck with me because you'll be lying next to yo homie when it's done!"

All Jay could do was laugh because at the end of it all, he still had love for Peanut.

"Nigga I could've smoked up bitch ass a long time ago, and if you don't watch yo mouth, I just might do it now," he said as he pulled his strap. James was on point as he pulled out his other gun. They was so caught up in each other that neither one of them noticed Peanut, Bubba D, and EJ as they snuck in the side door. They inched slowly towards the two as they argued. James froze and the cold steel kissed the back of his neck.

"You are so caught up in yo bullshit that you don't even notice the set up," said Peanut in his ear.

"Nigga, I know you didn't come in three deep and think you was gone survive," James said and then chucked.

"I took after my pops in more away than one. Of course, I know I got ya boys out here somewhere. The only thing is them bitches is slipping because I'm in here and they don't even know. Plus, I got shooters myself." He shot back with a smile. James looked at Jay because he knew the lil nigga had set him up.

"You snake ass…." Those were all the words he went to say as Peanut hit him behind the head with the butt of his gun. He slammed down his shit numerous times and as hard as she could. Once he saw blood squirt out, he eased up because he didn't want to kill him just yet. Jay saw in Peanut's eyes that he was in kill mode then sprinted towards the door, but Bubba D was on point and clipped him.. He felt flat on his face as Bubba D stood directly over him with his banga aimed at his head.

"I ought to blow your shit out for trying that dumbass shit!" Said Bubba D. Bubba D was pissed off by the little stunt that he pulled and started stomping him everywhere his feet landed. They were caught up in Jay trying to get away that they had forgotten about James' bitch ass. They were all stunned by the sound of a gunshot. Peanut looked around to see with one of them was shot. When he realized neither one of them was shot, he automatically knew what the gunshot was. He upped his heat just in time as the first nigga came through the doors. He shot at the nigga multiple times then dropped him a few feet in front of him.

Peanut heard shots coming from outside and knew that this crew was going hard on James' crew. Peanut saw Bubba D and EJ bursting at the side entrance smoking with everything the same though. He immediately thought about James and looked his way only to see that he was gone. Peanut quickly took off toward the back to look for him. He dove inside a side office as two bullets hit the wall next to him barely missing his head.

"You gon' be by yo daddy's side in a lil bit, lil nigga!" James yelled from somewhere.

When James said that it pissed him off to the max as he wanted him out. Peanut didn't realize how big the church was until now. He was regretting that this spot was chosen for the moment. He heard shot after shot coming from out back and up front. He wanted to be next to his homies but had to get at James bitch ass.

"Bring yo scary ass out and get this shit over with!" He yelled out. He saw James dash out and with the quickness, shot five times his way. James fell to the floor and Peanut was right over him with his gun in his face.

"Yo bitch ass ain't so bad now, is you? You a Pastor so you might as well start yo prayer right now," said Peanut.

James was shot in the leg and couldn't move so he was a Peanut's mercy. As he looked up at Peanut, he pictured Gray standing over him seeking revenge.

"If you gone shoot me, get it over with."

"Nigga you snake ass nigga. You killed my pops right in front of me and I didn't even know it was you," he said with tears in his eyes.

"FUCK YOU!" He yelled as he tried to spit.

Peanut pulled the trigga then emptied the rest of the bullets that was left in the chamber in his face.

"When you see my pops, tell him everything is all good now." He spit on him, kicked him then took off to get at Jay. When he got back up front, everything had calmed down so he made his way outside. He saw Bubba D, EJ, Papa, and some more niggas from his view, but the looked round to see if he spotted Jay.

"We lost the nigga homie," Bubba D said.

"How the fuck some shit like that happen?"

"Too much shit going on so we couldn't pay attention to him." They could see the anger in his eyes and understood how much it meant for him to get Jay.

"What about James?" Asked Papa.

"Hopefully, my pops get to get his revenge on him next," he said he made his way to his car. He took this time leaving because he knew the police wouldn't come due to Karen.

***

Peanut, Los, Karen, and Marisol sat at a round table in the backyard of Caesar's house, which was now Marisol's.

"Now that we got the main distraction out of the way, Los wants to be filled in," said Peanut.

"I want to be on y'all's team and help keep y'all's empire from falling, I know a lot of people on both sides and I'm sure y'all need the help," said Karen.

"Los, you now run the show but you never met the connect. Back in the day me and Karen use to have our own little thing going and along the way we made a few friends," explained Marisol.

"With our help, y'all can go to the top but y'all must never betray each other. We both love Gray so that messed up our friendship," said Karen.

Peanut and Los looked at each other and nodded their heads in agreement at what they were hearing. They both knew they could take over more than San Antonio and planned on doing just that.

"We accept y'all's offer and I promise everything on our end will hold up," said Los.

"We'll make sure y'all straight and never have to worry about nothing. I learned a lot from my pops and loyalty was one of them," he said giving Los dap. Before anybody could speak, Peanuts phone rang. He looked at the call and picked it up when he saw Hazel's number.

"What's up, lil mama?"

"My dad's funeral is about to start and we need a ride," she said.

"Alright give me like fifteen minutes and I'll be there," he said then hung up.

"We gotta go but we must celebrate a new beginning."

"Cool, hit me up later," said Los.

He stood up then gave him some love and hugged Marisol as him and Karen left for Pastor James' funeral. A million thoughts ran through his head as he planned his future as a top notch boss.

To Be Continued ...

Coming soon
Betrayal of a G II
A Gangsta's Revenge

Lock Down Publications and Ca$h Presents
Assisted Publishing Packages

BASIC PACKAGE	UPGRADED PACKAGE
$499	$800
Editing	Typing
Cover Design	Editing
Formatting	Cover Design
	Formatting
ADVANCE PACKAGE	**LDP SUPREME PACKAGE**
$1,200	$1,500
Typing	Typing
Editing	Editing
Cover Design	Cover Design
Formatting	Formatting
Copyright registration	Copyright registration
Proofreading	Proofreading
Upload book to Amazon	Set up Amazon account
	Upload book to Amazon
	Advertise on LDP, Amazon and Facebook Page

***Other services available upon request.
Additional charges may apply

Lock Down Publications
P.O. Box 944
Stockbridge, GA 30281-9998
Phone: 470 303-9761

Submission Guideline

Submit the first three chapters of your completed manuscript to ldpsubmissions@gmail.com. In the subject line add **Your Book's Title**. The manuscript must be in a Word Doc file and sent as an attachment. Document should be in Times New Roman, double spaced, and in size 12 font. Also, provide your synopsis and full contact information. If sending multiple submissions, they must each be in a separate email.

Have a story but no way to send it electronically? You can still submit to LDP/Ca$h Presents. Send in the first three chapters, written or typed, of your completed manuscript to:

LDP: Submissions Dept
P.O. Box 944
Stockbridge, GA 30281-9998

DO NOT send original manuscript. Must be a duplicate. Provide your synopsis and a cover letter containing your full contact information.

Thanks for considering LDP and Ca$h Presents.

NEW RELEASES

BLOODLINE OF A SAVAGE **BY PRINCE A. TAUHID**

THE MURDER QUEENS 4 **BY MICHAEL GALLON**

THE BUTTERFLY MAFIA **BY FUMIYA PAYNE**

KING KILLA 2 **BY VINCENT "VITTO" HOLLOWAY**

BABY, I'M WINTERTIME COLD 3 **BY MEESHA**

THESE VICIOUS STREETS **BY PRINCE A. TAUHID**

TIL DEATH 2 **BY ARYANNA**

CITY OF SMOKE 2 **BY MOLOTTI**

STEPPERS **BY KING RIO**

THE LANE **BY KEN-KEN SPENCE**

MONEY GAME 2 **BY SMOOVE DOLLA**

THE BLACK DIAMOND CARTEL **BY SAYNOMORE**

CRIME BOSS 2 **BY PLAYA RAY**

THUG OF SPADES **BY COREY ROBINSON**

LOVE IN THE TRENCHES 2 **BY COREY ROBINSON**

TIL DEATH 3 **BY ARYANNA**

THE BIRTH OF A GANGSTER 4 **BY DELMONT PLAYER**

PRODUCT OF THE STREETS **BY DEMOND "MONEY" ANDERSON**

Coming Soon from Lock Down Publications/Ca$h Presents

BLOOD OF A BOSS VI
SHADOWS OF THE GAME II
TRAP BASTARD II
By **Askari**

LOYAL TO THE GAME IV
By **T.J. & Jelissa**

TRUE SAVAGE VIII
MIDNIGHT CARTEL IV
DOPE BOY MAGIC IV
CITY OF KINGZ III
NIGHTMARE ON SILENT AVE II
THE PLUG OF LIL MEXICO II
CLASSIC CITY II
By **Chris Green**

BLAST FOR ME III
A SAVAGE DOPEBOY III
CUTTHROAT MAFIA III
DUFFLE BAG CARTEL VII
HEARTLESS GOON VI
By **Ghost**

A HUSTLER'S DECEIT III
KILL ZONE II
BAE BELONGS TO ME III
TIL DEATH II
By **Aryanna**

BETRAYAL OF A G | RAY VINCI

KING OF THE TRAP III
By **T.J. Edwards**

GORILLAZ IN THE BAY V
3X KRAZY III
STRAIGHT BEAST MODE III
By **De'Kari**

KINGPIN KILLAZ IV
STREET KINGS III
PAID IN BLOOD III
CARTEL KILLAZ IV
DOPE GODS III
By **Hood Rich**

SINS OF A HUSTLA II
By **ASAD**

YAYO V
BRED IN THE GAME 2
By **S. Allen**

THE STREETS WILL TALK II
By **Yolanda Moore**

SON OF A DOPE FIEND III
HEAVEN GOT A GHETTO III
SKI MASK MONEY III
By **Renta**

LOYALTY AIN'T PROMISED III
By **Keith Williams**

I'M NOTHING WITHOUT HIS LOVE II
SINS OF A THUG II
TO THE THUG I LOVED BEFORE II
IN A HUSTLER I TRUST II
By **Monet Dragun**

QUIET MONEY IV
EXTENDED CLIP III
THUG LIFE IV
By **Trai'Quan**

THE STREETS MADE ME IV
By **Larry D. Wright**

IF YOU CROSS ME ONCE III
ANGEL V
By **Anthony Fields**

THE STREETS WILL NEVER CLOSE IV
By **K'ajji**

HARD AND RUTHLESS III
KILLA KOUNTY IV
By **Khufu**

MONEY GAME III
By **Smoove Dolla**

MURDA WAS THE CASE III
Elijah R. Freeman

AN UNFORESEEN LOVE IV
BABY, I'M WINTERTIME COLD III
By **Meesha**

QUEEN OF THE ZOO III
By **Black Migo**

CONFESSIONS OF A JACKBOY III
By **Nicholas Lock**

JACK BOYS VS DOPE BOYS IV
A GANGSTA'S QUR'AN V
COKE GIRLZ II
COKE BOYS II
LIFE OF A SAVAGE V
CHI'RAQ GANGSTAS V
SOSA GANG III
BRONX SAVAGES II
BODYMORE KINGPINS II
By **Romell Tukes**

KING KILLA II
By **Vincent "Vitto" Holloway**

BETRAYAL OF A THUG III
By **Fre$h**

THE MURDER QUEENS III
By **Michael Gallon**

THE BIRTH OF A GANGSTER III
By **Delmont Player**

TREAL LOVE II
By **Le'Monica Jackson**

FOR THE LOVE OF BLOOD III
By **Jamel Mitchell**

BETRAYAL OF A G | RAY VINCI

RAN OFF ON DA PLUG II
By **Paper Boi Rari**

HOOD CONSIGLIERE III
By **Keese**

PRETTY GIRLS DO NASTY THINGS II
By **Nicole Goosby**

PROTÉGÉ OF A LEGEND III
LOVE IN THE TRENCHES II
By **Corey Robinson**

IT'S JUST ME AND YOU II
By **Ah'Million**

FOREVER GANGSTA III
By **Adrian Dulan**

GORILLAZ IN THE TRENCHES II
By **SayNoMore**

THE COCAINE PRINCESS VIII
By **King Rio**

CRIME BOSS II
By **Playa Ray**

LOYALTY IS EVERYTHING III
By **Molotti**

HERE TODAY GONE TOMORROW II
By **Fly Rock**

REAL G'S MOVE IN SILENCE II
By **Von Diesel**

GRIMEY WAYS IV
By **Ray Vinci**

Available Now

RESTRAINING ORDER I & II
By **CA$H & Coffee**

LOVE KNOWS NO BOUNDARIES I II & III
By **Coffee**

RAISED AS A GOON I, II, III & IV
BRED BY THE SLUMS I, II, III
BLAST FOR ME I & II
ROTTEN TO THE CORE I II III
A BRONX TALE I, II, III
DUFFLE BAG CARTEL I II III IV V VI
HEARTLESS GOON I II III IV V
A SAVAGE DOPEBOY I II
DRUG LORDS I II III
CUTTHROAT MAFIA I II
KING OF THE TRENCHES
By **Ghost**

LAY IT DOWN I & II
LAST OF A DYING BREED I II
BLOOD STAINS OF A SHOTTA I & II III
By **Jamaica**

LOYAL TO THE GAME I II III
LIFE OF SIN I, II III
By **TJ & Jelissa**

IF LOVING HIM IS WRONG…I & II
LOVE ME EVEN WHEN IT HURTS I II III
By **Jelissa**

183

BETRAYAL OF A G | RAY VINCI

BLOODY COMMAS I & II
SKI MASK CARTEL I, II & III
KING OF NEW YORK I II, III IV V
RISE TO POWER I II III
COKE KINGS I II III IV V
BORN HEARTLESS I II III IV
KING OF THE TRAP I II
By **T.J. Edwards**

WHEN THE STREETS CLAP BACK I & II III
THE HEART OF A SAVAGE I II III IV
MONEY MAFIA I II
LOYAL TO THE SOIL I II III
By **Jibril Williams**

A DISTINGUISHED THUG STOLE MY HEART I II &
III
LOVE SHOULDN'T HURT I II III IV
RENEGADE BOYS I II III IV
PAID IN KARMA I II III
SAVAGE STORMS I II III
AN UNFORESEEN LOVE I II III
BABY, I'M WINTERTIME COLD I II
By **Meesha**

A GANGSTER'S CODE I &, II III
A GANGSTER'S SYN I II III
THE SAVAGE LIFE I II III
CHAINED TO THE STREETS I II III
BLOOD ON THE MONEY I II III
A GANGSTA'S PAIN I II III
By **J-Blunt**

PUSH IT TO THE LIMIT
By **Bre' Hayes**

BETRAYAL OF A G | RAY VINCI

BLOOD OF A BOSS I, II, III, IV, V
SHADOWS OF THE GAME
TRAP BASTARD
By **Askari**

THE STREETS BLEED MURDER I, II & III
THE HEART OF A GANGSTA I II& III
By **Jerry Jackson**

CUM FOR ME I II III IV V VI VII VIII
An **LDP Erotica Collaboration**

BRIDE OF A HUSTLA I II & II
THE FETTI GIRLS I, II& III
CORRUPTED BY A GANGSTA I, II III, IV
BLINDED BY HIS LOVE
THE PRICE YOU PAY FOR LOVE I, II ,III
DOPE GIRL MAGIC I II III
By **Destiny Skai**

WHEN A GOOD GIRL GOES BAD
By **Adrienne**

A GANGSTER'S REVENGE I II III & IV
THE BOSS MAN'S DAUGHTERS I II III IV V
A SAVAGE LOVE I & II
BAE BELONGS TO ME I II
A HUSTLER'S DECEIT I, II, III
WHAT BAD BITCHES DO I, II, III
SOUL OF A MONSTER I II III
KILL ZONE
A DOPE BOY'S QUEEN I II III
TIL DEATH
By **Aryanna**

THE COST OF LOYALTY I II III
By Kweli

A KINGPIN'S AMBITION
A KINGPIN'S AMBITION **II**
I MURDER FOR THE DOUGH
By **Ambitious**

TRUE SAVAGE I II III IV V VI VII
DOPE BOY MAGIC I, II, III
MIDNIGHT CARTEL I II III
CITY OF KINGZ I II
NIGHTMARE ON SILENT AVE
THE PLUG OF LIL MEXICO II
CLASSIC CITY
By **Chris Green**

A DOPEBOY'S PRAYER
By **Eddie "Wolf" Lee**

THE KING CARTEL I, II & III
By **Frank Gresham**

THESE NIGGAS AIN'T LOYAL I, II & III
By **Nikki Tee**

GANGSTA SHYT I II &III
By **CATO**

THE ULTIMATE BETRAYAL
By **Phoenix**

BOSS'N UP I, II & III
By **Royal Nicole**

BETRAYAL OF A G | RAY VINCI

I LOVE YOU TO DEATH
By **Destiny J**

I RIDE FOR MY HITTA
I STILL RIDE FOR MY HITTA
By **Misty Holt**

LOVE & CHASIN' PAPER
By **Qay Crockett**

TO DIE IN VAIN
SINS OF A HUSTLA
By **ASAD**

BROOKLYN HUSTLAZ
By **Boogsy Morina**

BROOKLYN ON LOCK I & II
By **Sonovia**

GANGSTA CITY
By **Teddy Duke**

A DRUG KING AND HIS DIAMOND I & II III
A DOPEMAN'S RICHES
HER MAN, MINE'S TOO I, II
CASH MONEY HO'S
THE WIFEY I USED TO BE I II
PRETTY GIRLS DO NASTY THINGS
By Nicole Goosby

LIPSTICK KILLAH I, II, III
CRIME OF PASSION I II & III
FRIEND OR FOE I II III
By **Mimi**

TRAPHOUSE KING I II & III
KINGPIN KILLAZ I II III
STREET KINGS I II
PAID IN BLOOD I II
CARTEL KILLAZ I II III
DOPE GODS I II
By **Hood Rich**

STEADY MOBBN' I, II, III
THE STREETS STAINED MY SOUL I II III
By **Marcellus Allen**

WHO SHOT YA I, II, III
SON OF A DOPE FIEND I II
HEAVEN GOT A GHETTO I II
SKI MASK MONEY I II
By **Renta**

GORILLAZ IN THE BAY I II III IV
TEARS OF A GANGSTA I II
3X KRAZY I II
STRAIGHT BEAST MODE I II
By **DE'KARI**

TRIGGADALE I II III
MURDA WAS THE CASE I II
By **Elijah R. Freeman**

THE STREETS ARE CALLING
By **Duquie Wilson**

SLAUGHTER GANG I II III
RUTHLESS HEART I II III
By **Willie Slaughter**

BETRAYAL OF A G | RAY VINCI

GOD BLESS THE TRAPPERS I, II, III
THESE SCANDALOUS STREETS I, II, III
FEAR MY GANGSTA I, II, III IV, V
THESE STREETS DON'T LOVE NOBODY I, II
BURY ME A G I, II, III, IV, V
A GANGSTA'S EMPIRE I, II, III, IV
THE DOPEMAN'S BODYGAURD I II
THE REALEST KILLAZ I II III
THE LAST OF THE OGS I II III
By **Tranay Adams**

MARRIED TO A BOSS I II III
By **Destiny Skai & Chris Green**

KINGZ OF THE GAME I II III IV V VI VII
CRIME BOSS
By **Playa Ray**

FUK SHYT
By **Blakk Diamond**

DON'T F#CK WITH MY HEART I II
By **Linnea**

ADDICTED TO THE DRAMA I II III
IN THE ARM OF HIS BOSS II
By **Jamila**

YAYO I II III IV
A SHOOTER'S AMBITION I II
BRED IN THE GAME
By **S. Allen**

LOYALTY AIN'T PROMISED I II
By **Keith Williams**

BETRAYAL OF A G | RAY VINCI

TRAP GOD I II III
RICH $AVAGE I II III
MONEY IN THE GRAVE I II III
By **Martell Troublesome Bolden**

FOREVER GANGSTA I II
GLOCKS ON SATIN SHEETS I II
By **Adrian Dulan**

TOE TAGZ I II III IV
LEVELS TO THIS SHYT I II
IT'S JUST ME AND YOU
By **Ah'Million**

KINGPIN DREAMS I II III
RAN OFF ON DA PLUG
By **Paper Boi Rari**

CONFESSIONS OF A GANGSTA I II III IV
CONFESSIONS OF A JACKBOY I II
By **Nicholas Lock**

I'M NOTHING WITHOUT HIS LOVE
SINS OF A THUG
TO THE THUG I LOVED BEFORE
A GANGSTA SAVED XMAS
IN A HUSTLER I TRUST
By **Monet Dragun**

QUIET MONEY I II III
THUG LIFE I II III
EXTENDED CLIP I II
A GANGSTA'S PARADISE
By **Trai'Quan**

BETRAYAL OF A G | RAY VINCI

CAUGHT UP IN THE LIFE I II III
THE STREETS NEVER LET GO I II III
By **Robert Baptiste**

NEW TO THE GAME I II III
MONEY, MURDER & MEMORIES I II III
By **Malik D. Rice**

CREAM I II III
THE STREETS WILL TALK
By **Yolanda Moore**

LIFE OF A SAVAGE I II III IV
A GANGSTA'S QUR'AN I II III IV
MURDA SEASON I II III
GANGLAND CARTEL I II III
CHI'RAQ GANGSTAS I II III IV
KILLERS ON ELM STREET I II III
JACK BOYZ N DA BRONX I II III
A DOPEBOY'S DREAM I II III
JACK BOYS VS DOPE BOYS I II III
COKE GIRLZ
COKE BOYS
SOSA GANG I II
BRONX SAVAGES
BODYMORE KINGPINS
By **Romell Tukes**

THE STREETS MADE ME I II III
By **Larry D. Wright**

CONCRETE KILLA I II III
VICIOUS LOYALTY I II III
By **Kingpen**

BETRAYAL OF A G | RAY VINCI

THE ULTIMATE SACRIFICE I, II, III, IV, V, VI
KHADIFI
IF YOU CROSS ME ONCE I II
ANGEL I II III IV
IN THE BLINK OF AN EYE
By **Anthony Fields**

THE LIFE OF A HOOD STAR
By **Ca$h & Rashia Wilson**

THE STREETS WILL NEVER CLOSE I II III
By **K'ajji**

NIGHTMARES OF A HUSTLA I II III
By **King Dream**

HARD AND RUTHLESS I II
MOB TOWN 251
THE BILLIONAIRE BENTLEYS I II III
REAL G'S MOVE IN SILENCE
By **Von Diesel**

GHOST MOB
By **Stilloan Robinson**

MOB TIES I II III IV V VI
SOUL OF A HUSTLER, HEART OF A KILLER I II
GORILLAZ IN THE TRENCHES
By **SayNoMore**

BODYMORE MURDERLAND I II III
THE BIRTH OF A GANGSTER I II
By **Delmont Player**

BETRAYAL OF A G | RAY VINCI

FOR THE LOVE OF A BOSS
By **C. D. Blue**

KILLA KOUNTY I II III IV
By Khufu

MOBBED UP I II III IV
THE BRICK MAN I II III IV V
THE COCAINE PRINCESS I II III IV V VI VII
By **King Rio**

MONEY GAME I II
By **Smoove Dolla**

A GANGSTA'S KARMA I II III
By **FLAME**

KING OF THE TRENCHES I II III
By **GHOST & TRANAY ADAMS**

QUEEN OF THE ZOO I II
By **Black Migo**

GRIMEY WAYS I II III
By **Ray Vinci**

XMAS WITH AN ATL SHOOTER
By **Ca$h & Destiny Skai**

KING KILLA
By **Vincent "Vitto" Holloway**

BETRAYAL OF A THUG I II
By **Fre$h**

BETRAYAL OF A G | RAY VINCI

THE MURDER QUEENS I II
By **Michael Gallon**

TREAL LOVE
By **Le'Monica Jackson**

FOR THE LOVE OF BLOOD I II
By **Jamel Mitchell**

HOOD CONSIGLIERE I II
By **Keese**

PROTÉGÉ OF A LEGEND I II
LOVE IN THE TRENCHES
By **Corey Robinson**

BORN IN THE GRAVE I II III
By **Self Made Tay**

MOAN IN MY MOUTH
By **XTASY**

TORN BETWEEN A GANGSTER AND A
GENTLEMAN
By **J-BLUNT & Miss Kim**

LOYALTY IS EVERYTHING I II
By **Molotti**

HERE TODAY GONE TOMORROW
By **Fly Rock**

PILLOW PRINCESS
By **S. Hawkins**

BETRAYAL OF A G | RAY VINCI

SANCTIFIED AND HORNY
by **XTASY**

THE PLUG OF LIL MEXICO 2
by **CHRIS GREEN**

THE BLACK DIAMOND CARTEL
by **SAYNOMORE**

THE BIRTH OF A GANGSTER 3
by **DELMONT PLAYER**

BOOKS BY LDP'S CEO, CA$H

TRUST IN NO MAN
TRUST IN NO MAN 2
TRUST IN NO MAN 3
BONDED BY BLOOD
SHORTY GOT A THUG
THUGS CRY
THUGS CRY 2
THUGS CRY 3
TRUST NO BITCH
TRUST NO BITCH 2
TRUST NO BITCH 3
TIL MY CASKET DROPS
RESTRAINING ORDER
RESTRAINING ORDER 2
IN LOVE WITH A CONVICT
LIFE OF A HOOD STAR
XMAS WITH AN ATL SHOOTER

www.ingramcontent.com/pod-product-compliance
Lightning Source LLC
Chambersburg PA
CBHW071205260626
47162CB00003B/1182